BLACKCOCK'S FEATHER

MAURICE WALSH

SCHOOL EDITION

LONGMANS, BROWNE AND NOLAN LTD.

This is a specially abridged
edition for use in schools. A full
library edition is available.

Printed in the Republic of Ireland by
Criterion Press Limited, Dublin

CHAPTER I

FROM MOUTH OF AVON TO DUBLIN TOWN

THIS is the story of me, David Gordon, and I will begin it on that day in May when I walked down the quay-wall at Mouth of Avon below Bristol and held discourse with one Diggory, sailing-master of the *Speckled Hind.*—I begin it on that day because it was on that day Life began for me.

The sailing-master stood wide-leg on his poop-deck, a short square fellow with a spade-beard below a leather basnet.* The grey-green waters of the Bristol sea shimmered and ran behind his wide shoulders ; the wing of a gull white-flashing in the sun flicked and dipped across the green, and the uncanny cry of the bird made mock of me and of all men. He was in converse with a tall young gallant who leant in a carelessly elegant pose against one of the caryatids, slim rose-hosed legs ankle-crossed and a gauntleted hand in the silken folds of slashed trunks.†

The shipmen were rolling casks of Spain wine on board, and the roll of the casks on the wooden shell of the quay had the quivering deep boom of a drum. I picked a road between them and stood on the edge of the wharf within a long stride of the wide rail of the poop.

The shipmaster glanced up at me from under his black brows and went on talking. I waited until he looked again. " Master," I called then, " a word with you ! "

The gallant facing him turned and his countenance surprised me. His back was the back of a court popinjay, but his face was the face of a man. Below the brim of a high plumed hat a bold blue eye looked out at each side of a

* A light headpiece of steel or leather. † With slits to show coloured lining or puffing.

3

strong bony nose, and lip and chin carried a trained but manly amber beard.

"Yourself it is?" greeted the shipmaster in his Cornish tongue. "You come early."

"A week past," I explained, "I engaged with you a passage for two men to Dublin town in Ireland."

"Ay! an' if you be aboard at run of tide come seven of the clock, in Dublin town you will be in three days in spite of the King o' Spain and the Waterford pirates."

"Now I need a passage for but one man."

"One let it be," said he, "and no questions asked."

"I paid you an English pound for each passage and would claim one back, if I might."

And at that the silken gallant threw up his head and laughed a gay laugh, a laugh with a fine ring.

"You laugh easily, sir," said I mildly.

"The only way to laugh." His was the light mincing tone of London Court. "I think, sir, that your nation is known to me."

"It is not, sir," said I. "I have no nation."

"As you please. Many of that breed there be and most of them finish in the same way—head on spike over a town gate."

"From hurting men in silk doublets."

"Touch, sir!" He threw up his gauntleted hand in the fencer's gesture. "Silk doublet I wear, and hurt I avoid without good reason.—Well, Master Diggory?"

Diggory the shipmaster looked at me, a gleam in his eye, and shook his head. "'Tis against the rule."

I was as reasonable as any man. "If 'tis so, it cannot be helped," I said. "But your rule is a dishonest one, whoever made it."

He mocked me with his great bellow of a laugh. "To tell truth," said he, "I made that rule myself this very minute."

I looked him over very carefully. Though his eyes were

merry there was a hot spark behind them. Now, a pound is a pound and I had not many left in my purse, but half Scot though I might be, it was not the gold coin that urged me on. It was the Gael in me that hated to be laughed at. " A rule made by one man," said I, " should be in the keeping of that man. If you are honest as well as Cornish you will be putting an addendum to it." That was a long speech for me.

" I might," said he, " if I could remember it."

" That any man who could get the unused fare back from you would be welcome to it."

" Surely," he cried. " That goes without saying."

The hot spark in his black eyes had not belied him. His type was known to me. In Picardy and the Walloons I had met many of his kidney ; squat fellows with great girth of chest, vain of their sheer strength, and despising and disliking tall men. Small hardy men I had met, too, who were always in the company of tall men and loved by them. Tall enough was I and at that time I did not think any man drawing breath was stronger. At the back of my mind I was sorry to be taking advantage of this fellow's vanity and dislike.

He thrust a stained brown paw into his leather trunks and displayed a fat skin purse ; he shook it and it clinked richly. " Your coin is in there with others," he taunted. " Come and get it if you are able, long-shanks ! "

In two strides I was over the rail and on the poop. He was surprised at my readiness. With a ludicrous hurry he fumbled his purse into its hiding-place and backed away, one shoulder hunched forward and an elbow crooked, like a man used to wrestling.

I turned to the gallant still elegantly slouching against the caryatid and took off my fine Highland bonnet. " If it please you," I requested, holding it out to him. " I would not like that blackcock's feather broken."

He took the bonnet in the tips of his gauntleted fingers. " Better it than the broken head you will have in a trice," he warned. " Cornish men start wrestling in their infancy. Guard you ! "

Suddenly everything was quiet all round us. The rumble of the wine casks ceased and from the distance came the faint clang of chains on board one of William de Burgh's transport ships. And then the gull's cry again mocked us.

It was as I turned from the gallant that the shipmaster made his rush, head down like a bull. But just for that blind rush I had played. I slipped a bare step aside and as he went by dealt him a single thrust of hand and foot. He fell flat on his face, my knee was in his back—and before he could twist I had his purse in one hand and my pound in the other. And before he was on his feet I was over the rail and on the quay-wall. In sword-play, in wrestling —in Life—one has to be quick or eat dust, and in this small tussle slowness might mean mauling and blood-letting.

I held up the coin for him to see, whereat he swore terribly and made a rush for the rail. I threw his purse in his face, and shut-eyed he clutched at it. And there was my fine gallant facing him. " Your rule settled for you, my Diggory," he said.

The shipmaster tried to get by, but the gallant brought gauntleted hand-clap on shoulder, and his voice, no longer mincing, was sharp as hand-clap. " Enough, Master Diggory ! One addendum at a time. Enough, I say ! "

Diggory drew back growling ; on the wharf-wall a man laughed ; and the rumbling of the casks again made the air hollow. It was but a small incident after all and it was finished.

The gallant came over the rail with lithe grace and was facing me on the quay, holding my bonnet out in his finger-tips. " Your cock's feather would have run no risk," he said. " Might I have a word with you ? "

" If your road is mine," said I, who had no desire further to bandy words with him or with the irate shipmaster.

And so we went up the quay-wall side by side.

By habit I am a leisurely long-striding walker as one is who has spent years aimlessly, and this courtier-gallant had the light carriage of one used to picking his steps across polished floors. We were indeed no matched pair. He was tall and lithely slim ; I was taller and heavy shouldered above lean stomach. His silk hose and orange buskins, his slashed trunks and lace ruff, his short scarlet-lined cloak with rapier acock below it were a complete contrast to my sober cloth and leather, and plain black-hafted knife at hip. But I do think that my bonnet with blackcock's tail over one ear was a more gallant headgear than his high-crowned hat.

Also he was handsome and bearded, while I was clean-shaven and ugly. Ugly ! Ay ! Ugly I was and ugly I am : a dangerous sullen fellow to outward seeming, though in truth I was even then of mild and reasonable habit. My face belied me. It was a long hatchet face, a bony dour face, with red-brown eyes deep-set close to a lean nose, and dark-red hair waving back from a high jut of brow. No maid might look at me twice ; and men might count me dangerous, a man too ready for bare steel. Yet in all my twenty-eight years I had never pulled sword in anger, never drawn blood with point or edge, never sought a quarrel or made one. I was but a plain Highland clansman with a clansman's loyalty, used to following my father here and there in strange places and biding my time patiently.

This tall gallant gave me a sideways look. " What I would ask," said he courteously enough, " is why you seek passage to Ireland ? "

I considered that question. " If you have the right to ask that," I told him at last, " I will answer you with truth—or lie."

" As seems best to you. I am Francis Vaughan, Knight and Queen's Captain, brother-in-law to William de Burgh the new Lord Deputy of Ireland—a prudent veteran ! and any man who would set foot in Dublin these days must bear with his questioning."

"In that case, Sir Francis Vaughan," said I, "I will tell you that my name is David Gordon, out of Scotland, and that I go to Ireland to seek my fortune."

At that he halted his light stride and, with that gay habit of his, threw back his head and laughed pleasantly. And this time I halted with him and patiently let him have his laugh out.

"Your pardon," he excused. "But it is droll that a man should seek Ireland and a fortune at the same time." He let his eyes rove over me from heel to crown. "The only plenty in wild Ireland these days that might suit you is a plentitude of blows." He paused for a reply.

"I am no dealer in blows," I told him.

I saw by his smile that he did not believe me.

"In my Queen's Ireland you will deal or be dealt them. Quit me of offence, Master David Gordon, but back there on the *Speckled Hind* your treatment of hot Diggory was so featly managed that I am prompted to think you a dangerous man behind a sword—if you carry one."

"An Andrea Ferrara*, but—— "

"And it is well worth inquiring on which side you might use it."

"Sir," said I, "three days ago I could have answered your inquiry if I had a mind. But now I cannot."

He looked at me with puzzled scrutiny and then shrugged his shoulders. "Ah, well ! Let it be ! Your answer can wait. One other question. Who was the other for whom you had passage engaged ? "

"My father. I buried him yesterday in St. Werburgh's churchyard."

And that is why I begin my story on this day. For until my father died I was not the entity that is David Gordon. I was only my father's son, following him about in strange and lonely towns in France and the Netherlands.

---

* i.e., a sword made by Andrea Ferrara, an Italian armourer of the 16th century, whose name is found on many Scottish claymores or broadswords.

CHAPTER II

SWORDSMEN AT LARGE

MY father, tall and handsome Iain Gordon, was aye a wandering man, and a wandering man he died. He was younger son of Gordon of Auchindoun in Scotland, sept of Huntly, and he had two loves in all his life : my mother, who died in his arms at Auchindoun ; and his sovereign, Mary Queen, whose headless body he saw in the castle of Fotheringay. And that last love ruined his life and left me without a career.

In his early manhood he had gone adventuring with one of the MacNeill hired fighting-men into Dalriada and Clandeboye across the Irish Sea, and as far as the wild, half-royal, open-handed Court kept by Shane O'Neill, Prince of Ulster, at Dungannon. It was there that he met and became friendly with Donald O'Cahan, Chief of Ciannachta, and accepted an invitation to feasting at the O'Cahan stronghold of Dungiven on the Roe. And there, at Dungiven, he saw Fionnuala, daughter of the house, and his heart became entangled in the meshes of her red hair.

He was only a penniless younger son, and she the daughter of a chief who counted ten thousand head of kine and led five hundred gallowglasses into battle. But love does not calculate by beeves or battle-axes, and the two were secretly wed by a young Austin monk and fled to the protection of Sorley Boy MacDonnell in the Antrim fastnesses.

My father was at that last grim feast that Sorley Boy and his Scots gave the great Shane O'Neill in the Glens, a feast that began with boiled ox-blood and ended with daggers. Twenty black *scian* strokes went to the killing of the O'Neill, and the blood spilled that night was the first of an ocean. But for that long spilling my father did not tarry. He was one of the few who stood at the O'Neill's side that night, and again he had to flee. This time he brought his young wife home to Auchindoun.

There at Auchindoun was I born, and there my Irish mother died before ever I knew her. There for twenty years I lived the life of a Highland youth, coming to my many inches and shoulder-spread, as well I might in that clean Highland air ; learning little in book-lore but a goodly store from Nature. A Benedictine Father taught my cousins and myself a little Latin and some English and a fair theory of Christianity, but his lessons we were aye ready to forsake for a turn at the Fiddich river trout or at Huntly's deer, or for a bout of wrestling or claymore. A splendid fine youth, that of mine, if only I had realised the fact ! Youth never does. My hero-father had followed Mary of Scotland into English exile, and was in all the conspiracies to set her on one throne or on two ; he was away in a fairy-world playing gallant adventures, risking but never losing life in a Queen's cause, throwing a bold game against the English. And I would be with him in that romantic realm. How I longed to be with him ! And with him I would be as soon as beard stood up to razor's edge—as soon as I could swing broadsword in double cross. I was with him soon enough, and I was to be with him many weary days.

For Edinburgh and the new Church in Scotland had a long reach, and my " popish-plotting " father was none too safe even in the remote glen of the Fiddich. Moreover, his elder brother Alistair, now Laird of Auchindoun, was a prudent man who wanted no trouble ; saying few words, he nevertheless made plain that a long visit was not expected, and that any help that might be given must be given at a distance. My father took the hint and umbrage at the same time. Within a month he was out of Auchindoun and I with him, and a week after that both of us were at sea, and came to land at Dunkirk in France.

We were driven to many shifts. Aid from Auchindoun

was tardy and never princely. It did no more than eke
out what we earned precariously by our swords and our
sinew. By our swords ? So. I, that was so keen to wield a
soldier's blade, never wielded any but the sham one of the
fencer. My father, a skilled swordsman, taught fencing and
wrestling in small towns on the skirts of campaigning armies,
and I was his foil. Broadsword, broadsword and targe, rapier,
rapier and cloak, rapier and dagger in the new Italian mode
—I acquired some knowledge of them all and helped to teach
them in garrison towns. I had strength of wrist and weight of
shoulder-drive, but my father said I was clumsy, and might
be clumsier if the buttons were off or edge keened for blood
as it sheared. And, indeed, I met no real sworders to test my
skill.

Then there filtered to us, up from Spain or down from
Scotland rumours of the new fight the united Irish chiefs
were waging against Elizabeth. At first my father laughed
his grim unbelief. He admitted the fight, but was sceptical of
any unity of purpose. He had in mind the days of Shane
the Proud when O'Neill fought the O'Donnells, the Maguires,
the Scots of Clandeboye, anyone ; while the wily Sassenach
took this side and that side to ensure harmlessness by a general
ruin. Clan warfare was never done in Erin, and clan warfare
made no longer any appeal to a man who had plotted for a
queen.

But in time there could be no doubt that this new fight
was very nearly a national one. Hugh O'Neill, the queen-
made Earl of Tyrone, and young Hugh Roe O'Donnell of
Tyrconnell had brought all the North into a confederation
of power, had beaten the English in pitched battles, and were
threatening the very heart of the Pale—Dublin town.

So my father girded his loins afresh and a new light came
into his eyes. " There is work for us over there, David boy,"
he said. Somehow he still looked upon me as a boy, though
I was then in my twenty-eighth year. " Do not believe that
the Irish are backward fighters in their own land—as is held.

Nothing will stop a charge of gallowglasses but mailed horse, and only mailed horse have beaten them in open fight. This O'Neill is something more than an ordinary cut-and-thrust leader of wild lads ; he seems to have learned the arts of Burleigh and Walsingham* while he was at Greenwich Court. And it looks to me that there is good chance the fight will not stay in Ireland. The Highland tie is still strong and—who kens ? we might set a Scots king on an English throne without waiting for a dead woman's dancing shoes. Let us up and away. We have kin amongst the O'Cahan of Dungiven and we will look in on them."

So we crossed the French sea and by devious ways came to Bristol. And there the first thing we learned was that a truce had been made in Ireland and that there was full likelihood of a settlement with the northern chiefs.

My father, used as he was to disappointments, was hit deeply by the blow. Outwardly there was little sign of the wound ; but, I think, deep down his last hardihood was sapped. " Well, lad ! " he said patiently, " since we are so far on the road we will not turn back." And then a bitterness came into his tone. " But I might have guessed that clan chiefs—earls of a usurper queen—would not hold steady on one course."

So we went down to Avon Mouth to seek passage to Dublin. One was easy got. The new Lord Deputy to Ireland, Sir William de Burgh, was there outfitting his expedition and in addition to the Queen's squadron had impressed every seaworthy boat from Bristol and Bideford. These privateer shipmasters were glad enough to eke out the meagre official fee by a little private trade, and the first man we spoke struck a bargain for a brace of pounds—and lost one, as has been told.

* William Cecil, Lord Burleigh, Chief Minister to Queen Elizabeth ; and Sir Francis Walsingham, another of her statesmen. They were both instrumental in bringing about the execution of Mary Queen of Scots at Fotheringhay Castle, Northamptonshire, in 1587.

It was the beginning of May, and a cold north wind blowing down from the Welsh mountains nipped my father with his vitality at lowest ebb. He took to his bed with a shooting pain across the back, made no struggle, turned his face with a strange loneliness from me and the world, and was dead in five days. More than that I will not say.

But there I was at a loose end. No longer had I any living loyalty to uphold me, no hate to spur me, no clearly seen object to strive for. I was only David Gordon out of swaddling clothes, for all that I was a grown man—a big, long-legged, sullen lad without any of the enthusiasms of youth. And lacking these, life is a terrible thing for youth. What had I, then ? A purse of twenty gold coins, a long blade of Ferrara, and—nothing more. Once on a time I would have asked for nothing better than a loose foot and that blade to carve a road. But now I knew too much, or I did not know enough. I had to choose my road, and there was no choice that called me like a trumpet.

I could go back to Auchindoun and live the life of a kinsman to a small laird, with a faint prospect of a small place in Edinburgh, and a still fainter one of following James Stewart,* that unnatural son, to London town ; I could go back to the walled town of Arras where a certain colonel of pikes had employ for strong shoulders ; or I could, no doubt, get a place in this expedition to Ireland, since this Sir Francis Vaughan might be glad of a volunteer, it being evident that the pressed train-bands of Somerset and Devon had no stomach for the work before them.

What else might I do ? Ah, well ! My father was scarcely cold in his grave and I would be no traitor to him. Let me be loyal for a little while yet and set foot on the road he had pointed. Very like there were cousins of mine amongst the

---

* James VI of Scotland, son of Mary, Queen of Scots. He made no serious attempt to save his mother from her fate. On the death of Elizabeth in 1603 he succeeded to her throne as James I of England, in virtue of his descent through his mother from the royal family of the Tudors.

O'Cahan near Derry Columcille, and, anyway, I could be moving in that direction without binding myself to any side in any quarrel. To Dublin town, then, would I go with a mind not yet made up.

It was in that lax spirit that I took passage for Ireland.

CHAPTER III

THE CITADEL OF THE PALE

I WENT down the quay-wall that evening shortly before seven of the clock, my not-too-heavy travelling-satchel slung on shoulder, light purse in breast of cloth doublet, and long Andrea Ferrara at left hip—loneliness in my heart, and none of the hopes of youth to leaven it. Sir Francis Vaughan was on the poop-deck with some of his officers. He now wore the sailor's leather head-piece and had changed his short scarlet-lined cloak for a long one of blue cloth. Both suited his soldierly face. The tide was full in, and he stood leaning on the rail, looking down at me. " Dublin town it is, then ? " he greeted, gesturing towards the gangway at the waist of the ship. " Come up this way ! "

The waist was crowded with buff-coated arquebusiers*, and the shipmen were hustling about amongst them at their duties, of which I am very ignorant. Already big brown sails were hanging loosely here and there, and a line of seamen up in the bow were tailing on a rope and marking time to a sea-song.

I was at the foot of the poop-stairs when a voice hailed me. " Hey, master ! One-piece passengers in the mainhouse."

It was Diggory the ship-captain. His eyes were black and he came at me with a power of truculence. One place was the same as another to me, so I turned away from the poop.

---

* Gunners. The arquebus was an early type of portable gun, supported on a tripod.

" This way, Master David Gordon," came Sir Francis Vaughan's voice from the stairhead. " My good Diggory, if you will attend to your business of casting-off I will attend to this gentleman for a little while."

Diggory glowered at him and then at me, a heat in his eyes.

" Man," said I peaceably, " forget you. A Cornish wrestler should take a fall as it comes."

" That was not fair wrestling."

" No. I was not wrestling that time."

He went off growling, and presently his voice came bellowing from the forepart of his ship.

I mounted the stairs to Vaughan's side. " The mainhouse is packed like salt fish," he said. " Doubtless there will be a corner up here."

I thanked him kindly.

He laughed his pleasant light laugh and, taking my arm led me aside to the rail away from his officers. " Do not flatter me," he said. " My kindness has its own meaning. A tall cool man who uses his head and wears a long sword has much to commend him—in this business we are embarked on. You are better on my Queen's side than against her."

" I am on no side."

" As you say. But who seeks fortune in Ireland has to be on one side or the other. Look, Master Gordon, and you will see on which side fortune is ! "

I looked out to sea, and the sea was crowded with sails— white and black and red sails, with the green English sea between and the gold path of the sun laid down amongst them.

" De Burgh's fleet," he said, " three thousand veteran soldiers, a couple of thousand stout lads of Devon and a park* of culverin."†

" And a truce in Ireland ! " My tone had a slight taunt in it.

He laughed. " Of a sort. The wild Irish must have their lesson this time."

" Or teach one ! "

* Space occupied by artillery.   † Large cannon.

" They might—as at Clontibret not so long ago. Here goes our answer to that, if need be. William de Burgh, fresh from fighting Spain, has a trick or two to astonish the O'Neill." He pointed into the waist of the ship. " There be some five standards of fighting-men down there, and you can have your chance of fortune if your mind leans that way."

Here was the direct offer. What would my father have said to that ? Nothing. It was not his custom to display his thoughts.

" My Queen is a good mistress," said Vaughan, quietly urging. " She has contended against your Scotland and Spain—and Ireland always, and has beaten them all."

" And men do not trust her."

" Any man that does—for his own ends, not England's —carries a loose head. But, Master Gordon, if you mistrust my Queen take this my offer as personal. To tell truth I was greatly taken with you and am honestly interested to see how you take to soldiering."

" I am no soldier," I told him.

" You carry a good long blade and a cool head."

" But I am no soldier."

" Be it so. Your attention, Master Gordon. No man like you, sword and habit, may go foot-loose about Dublin and out of it without question. That is only prudence and no threat. Pray consider my offer at your leisure and let us say no more for the present. Will you accompany me to the after-house and try a stoup of wine ? "

At that we left it.

I came out on deck on the third afternoon, and there was the Irish coast close at hand. A stiff headland thrust itself out into deep water, and behind it, above thick young-foliaged woods, two conical peaks stood up against the sky ; away in the north another heathery headland, ribbed with stone, had the sea beating white against its base ; and between the two was a flat curve of shore with the River Liffey flowing sluggishly between sand-banks—and the sunlight in a soft haze shining on the dark green of woods, the bright green of sea grass, and making gold of the barren sands.

Most of the fleet anchored in the bay, but the Lord Deputy's ship and a few others—including the *Speckled Hind*—carrying leaders, ventured the river passage to the Dublin quays. During the last mile the seamen had to take to the boats and tow, a slow business even with the making tide. It was near sunset before we tied up at Wood Quay, above a strong double square tower, and there at last was Dublin town before us on the south bank.

I had expected something outlandish and strange in this citadel of the English Pale ; but it looked no different from any other town of similar state that I had sojourned in : just a middle-sized place with a shelter wall to the quays, high roofs behind, and a scatter of houses on the north side of the river. Upstream from us a towered bridge of two arches crossed the water. There was every sign of a thriving sea-trade, comfort, thrift, and a hard-held security. This evening the town was in gala to welcome the new Lord Deputy ; flags flew, drums beat, silver trumpets sounded, and the populace was down at the waterside to see the show. The merchant, apprentice, and artisan dress was the same that I had seen at Bristol or Dover, and I realised that this city outside the bounds of "wild" Ireland was but an English town.

I left the ship as soon as I might, satchel on shoulder and sword at hip. Sir Francis Vaughan was busy, and moreover I did not want him yet awhile to order my bestowing. He saw me go and made no effort to stay me ; he but waved a gauntlet and called, " See you again, Master Gordon."

Making my way amongst the crowd, I had my first surprise, and one small twinge for my father's memory, for the tongue that was spoken around me was not English, but the Gaelic—my mother-tongue. My father and I, speaking together, had always used that tongue. Here now in Dublin, it was in general use—and, I believe, a cause of some complaint amongst the loyalists—a broader *blas* than I was used to and emphasised differently, but still homely and understandable, and yet it sounded strange to hear a man, attired in hose and jerkin and with the unmistakable round and ruddy face of the Saxon, use the wide vowel and the strong guttural.

I made my way through the press towards a turreted tower above a wide arch giving on a steep street of timbered houses. Close to a buttress on the quayside of the arch was the first man I could put finger on as Irish—a tall lean fellow with clean-shaven face and no head covering. His thick red hair was finely combed down on his neck and cut straight across his brows—brows set in a lour above eyes intent on arquebusier and halverdier disembarking on the quay. A long woollen cloak, with hood fallen on shoulders, was thrown back, and bare sinewy arms were crossed on a crotal* brown tunic that reached knee-cap after the fashion of our Highland kilt. He wore finely wrought horse-boots of yellow leather ; his woollen cloak was lined with orange silk, and there was gold and silver work on leather belt. A gallant, tall, grim lad ! He carried no weapon that I could see, but then no " wild " Irishman was allowed weapon within Dublin walls.

Sometimes now I wonder if Providence set that man there to wait for me—and for his fate.

I paused at his shoulder and addressed him in the Gaelic. " Would there be an inn up this street, friend ? "

He started, and surprise was in the deep-set eye he turned on me. He looked me up and down, and I waited his answer patiently. " Plenty," he said at last and shortly. And then thought better of it. " This is the street of wine taverns. There is the ' Crane ' close at hand for a full purse—— "

" And—— "

" The ' Pied Horse ' near King's Gate is an honest house."

" My thanks. This way ? "

For another moment he turned to look louringly at the

* A lichen, used for dyeing.

Queen's ships, and I saw his jaw muscles ridge and ripple. Then he shrugged his shoulders and turned with me. " I will show you," he said.

We walked up the slope of the nearly empty street side by side, his head short of mine, but his stride as long as my stride. No townsman this. Once I caught his glance turned aside on me in keen scrutiny. No doubt he was nationally curious about this tall, narrow-eyed, ugly fellow in the feathered bonnet, who spoke a strange Gaelic. I had come off a Queen's ship and wore a long sword, yet I did not seem to be of the ship's company or a Queen's man. Now I know that, running in his mind, was the thought that by careful questionings some of the information he wanted might be won from me. Listen to him, then.

" 'Tis said this new Lord Deputy—de Burgh—is a fighting man."

" The Spaniards held him that, 'tis said."

" Fine judges, by all accounts. And he with ten thousand soldiers in his tail ? "

" A good many."

" You would think there was never a truce in Ireland," he said something warmly. " Like enough ye will be for harrying us out of the glens before harvest."

" I am for harrying no one."

" In bad company you were, then."

I did not agree or disagree.

" Good it is to be prudent," he said a little tartly.

" Surely," I agreed.

" Silence is as good as truth and sometimes no worse than a lie. That saying might be known where you come from ? "

" It is."

" You are no Sassenach, then. Here we are now."

As we turned under the hanging sign of the " Pied Horse," in the shadow of the King's Gate, I happened to glance down the slope of street. Women and young people were at the windows waiting for the show, but the street itself was empty except for one man, and him I knew. He was Sir Francis Vaughan's body-servant, a big fair fellow out of Essex named Tom Pybus. He seemed to be in a great hurry, but his hurry had started as I turned my head. He passed by without looking our way, and I followed the Irishman into the wide low ordinary of the inn.

Here were only the jerkined Anglo-Irish landlord and a saffron-clad man carrying a fine head of flaxen hair. But though the inn was now empty there was not a room to be engaged, and the landlord intimated as much very bluntly, after a glance at my cloth and leather.

My young conductor flared, but his voice came slow and cold. " That is a lie, my fine fellow."

The landlord did not treat this man rudely. There was respectful fear in his eye, and his hands were apologetic. He protested that the almoner of the Garrison had foreengaged all his rooms for the officers of the Devon trainbands now disembarking, but the Irishman would not accept that excuse. He had brought me here for lodging, and lodging I would have.

" I dare not," cried the landlord, and then had a bright thought. " Quarters your friend will have if you say it, Lord O'More," he said humbly, " and that is as good as prison-cell for me. But you have my best room, and with your favour, a pallet—— "

" Do not trouble," I stopped him. " I will seek other quarters."

" And not find them," said the landlord, " as long as the Queen's soldiers are in garrison."

This Lord O'More looked at me, and there was that speculation in his eye that I noticed before. And then that grim face of his smiled pleasantly. " My name is Colum O'More," said he, " and this is my cousin Cathal O'Dwyer." The other young Irishman nodded his flaxen head.

I did what was required. " My name is David Gordon," I told him.

" Out of Scotland—the Fifth Province ? A long way you are from home, but our race is kin and you are welcome to share what is going."

The Gael in me responded. And so my very first night in Dublin was spent with two Irish fighting-men—it was plain that fighting-men they were—from beyond the borders of the Pale.

CHAPTER IV

COSBY THE KILLER AND THE CRIME AT THE INN

EIGHT days I spent in Dublin, and then Fate, dim mover of gods and men, set my feet on the road ordained. And in these eight days a friendliness grew between me and the two young Irishmen, or rather between the flaxen-haired Cathal O'Dwyer and myself. O'More, with his red hair and grim face and hot eyes, was not a friendly man. He was a man apart, using me for his own purpose, and his own purpose— his one purpose in life—was to hold his land against the English. No doubt he thought the company of a man who had come off a Queen's ship useful company in the inquiries he was making. He was in Dublin under licence for the apparent purpose of selling native-bred ponies ; but though he said little, and I said less, I soon gathered that his main object was to discover the strength and quality of the English reinforce- ments and their disposal. O'Dwyer and I, shoulder to shoulder, followed him about the city of Dublin to the louring Castle with its round bastions, to Greneville Keep, Ostman Gate, the Bull Ring, wherever the soldiers were bestowed ; and even I, a stranger, could see that the new army was only in temporary quarters, and that its ultimate disposal meant no good to the doubtful truce that existed.

Young Cathal O'Dwyer was a friendly lad and got behind my dourness and silent habit ; they did not repel him, because he understood them. He took hold of my arm, tossed back his fine flaxen hair, gave me the friendly lustre of his gray eyes, and talked gaily and openly. In a day or two he made me free of their camp beyond the wall, where a score or so of light wiry men guarded a great herd of ponies on the Fair Green, near the ruined abbey of St. Francis outside the Bull Ring Gate. He made it plain that whatever their secret business might be they were there to sell ponies ; and a very good sale they had, too, for their hardy animals—hairy beasts with good legs, a hand higher in the shoulder than the Highland pony.

During these eight days I saw nothing of Sir Francis Vaughan, nor did anyone meddle with us or accost us. Once or twice I saw Trooper Tom Pybus, and he with a certain stupidity avoided seeing me. I realised that I was keeping company with spies and was being quietly spied on ; but with something of fatalism I let myself drift, for I could not make up my mind and waited for something to make it up for me. Poor Colum O'More ! with your hot eyes and mind set on war, it might be that Fate in the by-going used you for that purpose before she snapped the string for you.

At no time did O'More or O'Dwyer put me a direct question as to my business in Dublin. No doubt they wondered, but it was against their tradition to show an impertinent curiosity. They waited for me to display my mind and I had none to display.

So I was being quietly watched by both sides.

Midday of a Saturday and the three of us at meat in the ordinary of the " Pied Horse."

Truly the tavern was enjoying full custom. The long table and the cross table were crowded and some small trestle dining-boards had been set in the low window alcoves. The landlord, a prudent fellow, had bestowed us at one of these, for he was none sure that hot Irish chiefs would suffer shoulder-rubbing with English officers. I saw no harm or insolence in these young Englishmen. Fresh-faced boys out of Somerset and Devon, raw to war and the ways of dominance, they were boisterous at table, but never discourteous. Rather were they full of curiosity, and looked with something akin to admiration on these fine bareheaded young chiefs who had silk lining to their cloaks, gold bosses on their belts, wrought silver on their finely made horse-boots—and no weapon better than the short black knife.

We were eating our small loaves of white bread with soup, when a loud arrogant voice from the door made us turn head. Two men had just come in. One was Sir Francis Vaughan in his courtier dress ; the other was a soldier in the panoply of war—ribbed morion* and fluted corselet above long boots—and he was showing his teeth in a laugh. His teeth were more noticeable than the laugh. They were strong white teeth, and there was no chuckle of gaiety in the laughter. A superbly tall fellow he was, with upright carriage of head, great shoulders and flat stomach, flaxen moustaches curling up on his ruddy cheek-bones, and eyes so light that they looked like polished bosses of limestone. A man who, you would say at a first glance, was handsome and merry—and be only a good judge of looks.

" 'Sdeath ! the place is thick with shavelings." He said that loud enough for the room to hear.

I turned back to my soup. It was not my part to notice Vaughan, and the loud-voiced man did not interest me. I heard their footsteps come across the floor towards us, but there was no room for any others at our table. A heavy stride stopped close behind my chair, and the loud voice spoke again with contempt in it. " Dublin town's come to a nice pass, Vaughan ! Wild Irish at meat with English officers ! To your feet, dogs ! "

He addressed O'More across the board, and O'More took it well. His cheek-bones hardened and his eyes narrowed, but he made no move, and his voice was cold and quiet. " Our table, foul-mouth," he said in the Gaelic.

The man behind me, as I now know, was a veteran of

* An open helmet.

Irish wars and knew the language. " Ho ! Ho ! " There
was no merriment there. " Stop that dog's gibberish and lap
your wash in the corner.—You, too, leather-jerkin ! " His
hand clapped my shoulder and gripped.

O'More was swifter than I was. A mazer* of mead was
close to his hand, and in one rapid motion he caught and
flung it, vessel and liquor, at the fellow's face. The bully,
for all his size, must have been as quick as a cat. I felt a few
spatters of moisture, and then heard the vessel clank and roll
on the floor behind him. And before I heard that I heard the
rasp of steel out of scabbard. The soldier was as quick
as that. Oh, but he was deadly quick. For he slew the
unarmed Irishman then and there. O'More had not time to
push back the heavy chair before the sword-point was at his
face. The killer knew swording. He feinted quickly at the
eyes, brought O'More's arms up, and ran him through the
neck—a fierce thrust and recover that sent chair and man
over backwards and wrenched blade free.

A great, terrible, wordless cry filled the room. It came
from Cathal O'Dwyer. But I had no time to pay any attention
to Cathal O'Dwyer. Clumsy my father had dubbed me, and
yet Andrea Ferrara was bare in my hand as I twisted to my
feet, and the killer's sword was no more than on the recover
before I had shortened blade and lunged above the gorget.

He parried it in time and no more. My point ripped his
leather collar as he swayed away. " You, too," he cried, his
teeth a-grin, and he was too busy to say more for a space.

I drove in on him, all the will and force, every atom that
was of me and in me gathered to a point. The buttons were
off the blades and here was killing. " Kill him ! Kill him
before these Sassenach kill you." Something shouted that
through my head loud as thunder, and all that was David
Gordon became a close-set vigour behind a driven sword-
point.

A chair fell over, a table slithered, the blades grated and

* Wooden goblet.

twisted, I drove him. And there was his throat. My point pinged on the edge of his steel corselet and curved half-circle. The shock threw him back on his heels and his weapon was only at half-guard. I beat it aside, twisted in the upper circle, and made sure of his open mouth. And even as my blade lunged it was beaten fiercely upward, and Sir Francis Vaughan was between us.

It was as rapid at that. Not as much as half a minute —and in another second—— That second was over now and he was still alive, but my concentration still held. I was so sure that I was to die in that room under the swords of the English that now I swung to face them, sword on guard and feet set. No one made any move at all. All these young officers stood or sat crouchingly, shocked surprise and anger in their eyes ; but their eyes were not set on me. They watched that big brute of their own, and here and there came a murmur that was on the brink of the fighting growl. I might have known. It is only the veteran in Ireland, embittered by endless and very deadly fighting, by intrigue, by the constant strain of maintaining supremacy over a breed not at all suppressible, that acquires an unnatural brutality—a ruthlessness that has much of fear in it. This war in Ireland was not a gallant affair.

I turned to Sir Francis Vaughan. His back was to me as he faced O'More's slayer. Then someone came at my side and I heard a hard-drawn breath. Cathal O'Dwyer was crouching at my hip, his hand in the breast of his saffron tunic and his eyes on Vaughan. I knew he carried a long *scian* under his armpit and was going to kill or be killed. I caught him at the elbow and pulled him upright against my shoulder. " Not yet," I whispered. " Not now."

He looked upward into my face, a terrible agony in his eyes. " Let me die," he whispered back. " Let me die now."

I shook him. " We will kill him at the World's End."

He relaxed against me, and we heard Vaughan speaking.

"This is not finished, Captain Cosby." His voice was strong. "You will hear of it—— "

"Only spawn, Sir Francis!" His voice was as loud as ever, but his cheeks twitched and were ashen.

Vaughan stamped his foot. "You are under arrest. Hold yourself at the Castle until word comes from de Burgh. Go, now."

And Cosby went, thrusting his sword stained as it was into sheath and throwing his head up in bravado. Vaughan pivoted so that he was still between us, and the big fellow looked back at me over his shoulder.

"Another day, you dog," he threatened.

I said nothing, but at that instant I could have told him out of some strange vision that his life was for my plucking when the time came.

The room was watching me now—Vaughan and me facing each other. We looked each other full in the eye and said no word. So bitterly did I feel that I was ready to cross swords with this gallant and try my best to spit him.

His eyes left mine at last and looked behind me at the floor. "Will you see to your friend, Master Gordon?" he requested quietly.

There was no more to be said and nothing else to do.

CHAPTER V

THE MOURNING OF THE CLAN

UPSTAIRS in our room poor Cathal O'Dwyer, grinding one hand into the other, bent over the couch whereon lay the body of Colum O'More under silken-lined cloak. " O God ! O God ! O God ! " He spoke low and desperately. " What will the clan say ? How will I tell the clan ? "

" What will your clan do ? " I put to him.

A red flame leaped in him for a moment. " A thousand will die for this." But the desperate mood flowed over him again. " But he is dead—dead—and nothing matters. Why did we not die killing, David Gordon ? "

" Easy enough to die in Dublin town, brother, but not killing ! "

The door behind us opened and shut, and Sir Francis Vaughan was in the room. We turned and faced him. " I am grieved that this happened," he said at once, his high-crowned hat in his hand.

" Why did you beat up the sword at its work, Sassenach ? " Cathal cried at him, his hand coming up to his breast.

Vaughan looked at me. " I am sorry for that too," he told me and seemed anxious that I should know his motive. " What else might I do ? I saved Captain Cosby's life, but I saved yours, too. This is Dublin town, and if you had killed him, not even de Burgh could have saved your head from Hanging Gate."

This was true enough, but I was not in the mood to acknowledge it. "Who is this man Cosby?" I asked him bluntly.

" Captain Sir William Cosby, Governor of Cong and Hy-Many in Connacht."

Surely. We could tell him the names of all the Connacht loyalists who had hasted to Dublin for a council with the new Lord Deputy : Sir Conyers Clifford, Bingham of Galway, Clanricard, Dunkelin, O'Connor Roe, and the killer Cosby.

The dead man had gleaned that knowledge and was beyond all use of it.

"You will forgive me for intruding," Vaughan said then, "but I would warn you that you are no longer safe here." He looked at O'Dwyer and spoke shortly. "You, O'Dwyer, had better be back in your hills with your men and horses—and your chief there.—And for you, Master Gordon." He paused. "You have been keeping unsafe company, but I have three choices to offer you——" He paused again, and I waited patiently. "The first ship out of Dublin, a strong lodging in Bermingham Tower, or—the third choice you know."

Even as he spoke I had made my choice—and it was none of his three. But I had learned to hold my tongue in narrow places, and I but gestured towards the couch. "No place for choosing," said I. "To-morrow——"

"To-morrow I leave for Portmore in the Gap-of-the-North, and Cosby has the ear of de Burgh. To-morrow you may have no choice."

"To-morrow you will know my choice," I said evenly.

He looked at me long and steadily, as if trying to get behind the ugly mask of my face. "Let it be," he said at last, shrugging his shoulders. "You have a strong sword-arm, but it is not as long or as strong as my Queen's. She will hold you within the Pale or thrust you outside it as it pleases her, and I warn you not to be rash. We hold you securely Master Gordon."

Without another word he turned on his heel and left us. Now I knew where I stood. He had given me my orders. The stakes were on the board and the dice loaded, and I set my dour Scots jaw against compulsion.

Within an hour I went out of Dublin by the Bull Ring, behind the last of Colum O'More. He lay under his cloak on a bier borne by four men of his clan. Cathal O'Dwyer and his kerns marched behind, and Dublin town looked on, silent and aloof. I brought up the rear. I was without sword or cloak, and carried my feathered bonnet in my hand, for all men to see that I had no other motive in going beyond the walls than respect for a man who had befriended me, a stranger. But Andrea Ferrara, that dumb one that knew only one tune, lay by the dead man under his cloak, and my travelling satchel was hidden there too. It was well. Near Audeon's Gate I saw the man Pybus out of the tail of an eye, and knew that he would follow as far as he might. With the help of God I would lead him far and hard.

Never did I see men more stricken than the Irish kerns in their camp outside St. Francis Abbey. They made no wailings, but their shoulders were shrunken, their heads bowed, and their voices, that had been so gay always, had a quiet sombre depth more grievous than tears. But now and then, one and another looked up at Dublin Wall with its Hanging Tower louring down, and jaw muscles clenched and a long breath lifted sunken shoulders. God help this English town if ever it lay at the mercy of the Glens !

In the short time that had elapsed since the death of the young chief the camp had already been broken, the gear collected, and the pack-ponies loaded. By nightfall these men would be back on the hills ; to-morrow all the Glens would know ; next day no man of the Pale would be safe south of the Dodder river.

For a space Cathal O'Dwyer was busy with his camp affairs and I moved about by myself. I loitered back by the Fair Green, keeping an eye lifting, and saw no sign of Tom Pybus or any man I could put down as English. But as I watched behind a booth a small troop of horse came clattering out of the Bull Ring Gate and took the south road towards the first green lift of the hills. I stood looking after them. That was the kerns' road, too. These soldiers might have no concern with me, but they were on one of the roads I might go, and must be considered along with another road that might be guarded. So considering, I walked back to the camp and found Cathal O'Dwyer waiting for me.

Already he was a changed man. The killing had shocked
his soul off balance. He was no longer the gay lad with the
flaxen locks a-toss and the laughing grey eye. There was no
colour in his face, and his eyes were sunken ; life seemed to
have receded deep down in him. " We are ready now, David
Gordon," he said, his voice drawing slow and toneless.
" You will come with us ? "

" No, Cathal," I told him.   " I go another road," He
looked towards Dublin.

" I am not going back," I told him. " I go north."

" North ! "   He livened a little at the word.   " Where
Freedom is. Ah ! but it is a long road and the Gap is well
guarded."

" It is the road I go. I will tell you now that I am half
Irish. My mother was an O'Cahan of Dungiven. I go there."

" A strong clan. Young Donal Ballagh the chief is a namely
man. Always I knew that you were one of our own. Listen,
friend ! My life hangs by a thread. I should have died back
there. See the men's eyes when they look at me. This night
my life may be asked and given. Given—that is easy ! "

I put my hand on his shoulder. " Come with me, then."

" No, I must face the clan. It is the law. If I do not die
I will be a wandering man till I kill Cosby. That is the law
too." He looked close into my eyes. " If you meet him, do
not kill him unless you are pressed and I am dead. Word
will come to you wherever you are, and if my work is undone
I put it on you, blood brother."

" I take it," I said firmly, and went on. " I want you
to arrange the payment of my reckoning at the ' Pied Horse,'
and I want you to sell me a horse and a cloak—— "

" Anything the clan owns is yours. If fair play was given
you—*Mhuire !* only another second and you had him.
What is the good ; what is the good ? He is dead and my
heart withered. Come, brother."

He chose me a chestnut-red mare, five years old and fifteen-
and-a-half hands at the shoulder, broad-backed with good legs.

" Her name is Benmee," he told me, his hand in her
black mane, " and she is trained to arms. The longest day
she will carry you and the spark not quenched in her. Ride
her with the knee only and use her mouth softly. I trained
her that way to leave a man's hands free for hilt. You will
grow fond of her."

Fond and fond of her I grew, many a long day.

And then he fitted me with the dead man's travelling-
cloak. Alas ! the yellow-lined one that covered him had his
life-blood stains on it. The travelling-cloak of the Irish is
the finest campaigning-cloak I know. This one of mine
was of close-woven wool, dyed crotal brown and lined with
marten skins. Tall as I was, it fell from neck to heel, was of
generous width, and carried a hood to pull over the head in
night camp.

Cathal would take no money other than what was required
to pay my tavern reckoning, and I dared not press it on him.
At the end he led me to the edge of the camp and, as I sat on
Benmee, placed his hand on my thigh and looked into my
eyes. " The knowledge is in me that we will meet again,
David Gordon," he said. " Where or how, I do not know.
Listen, now. Make your own road north, keeping to the by-
ways and woodpaths." And thereupon he advised me closely
on the long way I must go and the dangers to be faced. At
the end he pressed my thigh. " Trust no man who lives
in a stone dún," he said ;   " but men who sleep in *bothans*
you can trust for one night or for longer—if they are on
the right side. Once across the ford at Portmore you are
in O'Neill's country and may ride openly any road, and no
one to challenge you, and you riding in peace. That is
all I can tell you, David Gordon—and if God is good to me
we will meet across the Shannon."

His was the wine of advice.

CHAPTER VI

BLACKCOCK'S FEATHER TRIUMPHS OVER THREE

BEHOLD me, then, that pleasant afternoon in May weather, riding my strong-backed chestnut-red Benmee westwards through the open woods along the Esker ridge* outside Dublin, my knees a-grip back of her elbow and her long shanks wagging comfortably. I rode the Irish saddle, which is stirrupless and no more than a felted pad girthed behind the withers. I was at home on such a saddle. All my youth I had ridden the Highland pony barebacked, and knew the art of leaning-back balance on easy roads and the grip of knee that gives the arms free play.

At last I was my own man going my own road, a good mare between my knees, a fine sword in hand, money in my purse, a long cloak against the night, food for two days— oaten bannock and collops of veal—and adventure beckoning me on the road. I was in tune with the sun and the spring, and my heart lifted with the blackbird's song.

For the first half-dozen miles I kept within the fringes of the woods—oak trees in early leafage mixed with the dark plumes of pine and the still budding boughs of ash. When at last the Esker slanted to the River Liffey I went still more warily, for here the risk began. From the shelter of the trees I examined the ground I had to go over. A slope of grass ran down to a ford, and beyond it a thick clump of sallies grew down to the edge of the water. Behind that the brae, heavily wooded, rose steeply and the green solid curves of the tree-tops fringed the blue of the sky.

I looked upstream and down. There was no one in view.

---

* The Esker Riada, a long natural wavy ridge, formed of gravel, running across almost the whole country from Dublin to Galway ; much celebrated in old times as a line dividing Ireland into two equal parts.

Now was the time. I gave Benmee a touch of knee, rode boldly down the slope and splashed into the water.

And as I splashed out on the other side a big man on a big horse came out from behind the sallies directly in my path. And the big man was Trooper Tom Pybus, dressed for war—buff coat, peaked casque, and long sword—but the sword was still in scabbard. And as I brought Benmee to a halt two more troopers edged out of the clump. Three to one ! Vaughan had given me good measure and flattered my prowess. Three to one, and back to Dublin city and worse ! It looked like that.

Pybus was a plain Saxon man and not given to heroics. He saluted me with a decent show of respect. " My master, Sir Francis Vaughan," said he, " wants word with you, Master Gordon, in Dublin town."

I kept my hands still, though my heart beat, and looked about me. There were no more than the three. Three were enough surely ; yet it was well for me that Vaughan was not come himself. My plight was desperate enough, but the notion of being led back to Dublin like a sheep never entered my head. I think that I was, somehow, glad that the test had come. For eight years I had been moribund, and now I was alive, and life was worth the risk. Here was the risk surely.

One thing I had learned in eight years wandering : that a man does not go far if action lags behind decision. I said no word at all. Tom Pybus, towering above me on the slope, a slow man on a heavy English horse, waited patiently for my answer, already sure of it. He got it, and it surprised him.

My blade was out of scabbard and poised in one long draw that had the song of steel in it. My knees pressed Benmee, and gallantly she responded, ears back and neck forward. She charged up the slope directly at the big horse, and Pybus had no time even to yell. Instinctively he pulled his off-rein and clawed for his hilt, and he was still clawing as I brushed by him. My blade was up and on the swing,

2

3

back-hand—that terrible late cut that has no guard and shears heads like a lad shearing thistles—but I did not shear the head of Tom Pybus. Instead, I let the flat of the blade come not urgently across his buff shoulders, and rode on.

I heard a bark of laughter from one of the troopers, and looked back over the curve of a shoulder. One was laughing indeed as he swung his horse awkwardly, but the other was wrestling with the lock of an arquebus. I crouched over Benmee's withers and gave her voice and rein, and she took the slope like a bird. We were near the head of it when the bellow of the shot roared amongst the trees. It was badly aimed, for I did not hear the whistle of the lead, and not even a leaf fell.

And that finished that small adventure.

Benmee and I had no difficulty in evading the pursuit, if pursuit there was. We were westwards of the cultivated lands round Dublin, and all that Meath border was thickly wooded and in places marshy. The heavy English horses lacked pace in such a country, and we soon got beyond sight and sound of them. Still we hurried, with the sun at my left shoulder, and never slackened till we got down on the soldiers' road to Trim. That we crossed safely after a careful scrutiny. By then the sun was behind the trees ; and the sky was red with the death of the day when we came to a strong stream gurgling between low banks of grass and iris. This, I judged, was the Tolka, and we crossed it and followed it up in the direction we were going till we came to a clump of larch in young foliage. We were now well away from all roads, and here I decided to camp.

First I unsaddled and unbridled Benmee, and let her roll herself fresh on a patch of dry soil. Then I tied her out to nibble a patch of short grass near the water, while I sat down on the bank to eat my supper frugally—one bannock and a rib of veal. As I ate I watched her mouth the grass daintily and switch her long black tail. I must be kind to this bonny mare of mine.

After supper I groomed her and, now that she was cool, led her to drink and thereafter plucked fresh herbage for her. By then it was full dusk, and I tied her out on the fringe of the larches and myself went in amongst the trees. Wrapped from neck to heel in my fine cloak and with the hood drawn up, I lay on my back in the fork of a root and looked up along the lean trunk at the dim crown of the tree, through which a star glinted down from a far-away pale sky. And I reviewed my day. Life had begun for me at last. Twice that day I had drawn sword—and my sword was still clean. I was not sorry for that now. All my old weary life—or lack of life—was behind me, and to-morrow I would start life afresh, facing strange and twisty roads with I-knew-not-what at the end of them. But if there was fight against the English, in that fight would I be ; and if fortune came my way, I would take it ; and if death took me, I would hope to be no craven, for death is a soldier's part and his meed, and no soldier should hope to draw old breath. David Gordon, fighting-man ! That was I.

There was no breath of air, yet the fronds of larch sighed to themselves, and here and there in the wood were small sounds of the life of small things—a quiet sigh, a quiet rustle— and quietly I fell asleep.

I wakened in the late dawn to the blackbird's song, a clear strong whistle that drowned the finches' chatter. Long unused to camping in the open, I was stiff and chilled, and the wan light of day-before-the-sun put something of sombreness on me. But the blackbird's song had a stir to it, and in a minute the mavis came trilling, and I was heartened to take the drastic course to make blood run freely. I stripped and plunged into a pool, let the runnel of a small cascade pour over me, and came out to run along the bank and slap myself till I was dry and glowing. Breakfast, then, and the saddling of Benmee, who was lively and already beginning to know me. And so I turned head northward and away.

CHAPTER VII

ANOTHER VICTORY

I TOOK all of eight days to reach the Ulster border—
O'Neill's line—on the Blackwater beyond Armagh. By the
soldiers' road to Dundalk and the Gap-of-the-North it might
be done in three ; but following O'Dwyer's advice, I kept
well wide of all made roads and steered a course of my own
by the sun. I was in no great hurry, and canny going was safe
going. Moreover, the line I took was no easy one. Mostly it
lay through a wilderness of heavy woods, thick undergrowth and dangerous green marshes. Here was a land
that was fast going back to a wild state after forty years
of ravage by raid and counter-raid. Time and again, following a faint track, I came on the ruins of townships sinking
down into the clay and grown over with brambles. In no
place at all did I come on any real sign of husbandry. Like
all races who live hardly and in constant peril of war, the clans
had become pastoral. They lived by their herds and on their
herds and on the game produce of the woods.

I avoided all habitations until my store of provisions
was finished, for it was well to get as far as I might from
Dublin before putting my kind to the test of hospitality.
On the forenoon of the third day, in a lumpy country of
bare knolls and marshy hollows, somewhere on the borders
of Uriel, I made my first venture. I struck a narrow kine-
trodden track with peat-moors on one side and stunted
pine-woods on the other, and followed it up. It wound in
and out on sound ground among quaggy marshes, and in
time rose up over the shoulder of a stony knoll. And from there
I looked into a small cup of a valley with pasturage on the
brae-side and cultivated patches in the hollow—a quiet and
pleasant small valley, sleepy under the midday sun. At the

far end, under a beetle of rocks, was a township of, maybe, a score of clay bothies, strung out in one straggling line.

Any stranger coming into that valley had to come by road and could be seen in good time by watchful eyes. Even as I rode over the knoll a man came out before the street and stood watching, and here and there women and children disappeared into black doorways. The man waited for me, and he was the only man in sight. A tall old fellow he was, wearing a crotal* tunic, cross-strapped trews, and rawhide brogans; with a lined worn face below shaggy grey hair, and one of his ears split in two by an old wound. He stood looking up at me; and sitting at ease—yet warily—on Benmee's broad back, I looked down at him. I gave him good-day, and in return he gave me God and Mary's blessing.

" Friend," said he, then. " Is there any news with you ? "

" Not a word," said I. " Is there any with yourself ? "

" Indeed no. Maybe you could tell us if they have struck in at the fighting—the Sassenach."

" The truce still holds."

" But not for long by all signs." He threw his hand back towards the bothies. " There is not a man left in the street— if it is men you are looking for."

" I am looking only for my dinner, father."

" To that you are welcome surely," he said readily. " There is the hind-quarter of a bull-calf in the pot, and a man's share and a guest's share is yours and welcome. Come down off your fine mare, tall hero."

So I lighted down, keeping an eye on the house doors. Here and there women peeped out, and children looked round their hips. No men, not even old men, did I glimpse.

" We will put the mare in the park," said my host.

The park was one of two stone-fenced fields in the bottom of the valley. It grew a short green herbage, and Benmee whinnied as she saw it. Leaving saddle and bridle slung on the fence we walked back to the old man's house. It was no

* A lichen from which a red dye is made.

larger than any of the others, though I gathered he was chief man and Brehon-judge of the village.

I bent head under the low lintel behind him, entering into the half-light.

I ran no risk at all. There was a peat-fire in the middle of the floor, with a big black skillet a-bubble on a crock over it, and from it a fine odour of veal and peat. There was a layer of smoke four feet off the ground ; a trickle of it came through the doorway, and a small trickle of it went up through the black-edged vent in the roof. There were a trestle-bench, a few stools, a round boss of stone, a block of bog-oak, and no other furnishing that I could see. And of people there were an old crone, a young pleasant-faced woman, and three sturdy half-clad children. They sat crouching out of the smoke, and I did likewise as soon as I might. And they made me welcome.

Into a big wooden dish on the trestle-bench the young woman poured the smoking contents of the black skillet, and there was, not one, but two quarters of veal. And we all sat round and ate, and sopped the gravy with bannocks of bread. The guest got first choice, and took it as a guest must, cutting off a browned slice high up on the thigh with his short *scian*, and passing the knife to the old man, who chose the next best cut judiciously. And in a short while there was nothing left but two long bones, and these a brindled hound took out of doors, where presently we heard him fight furiously with a brother.

We Gaels were always famous eaters of meat. At that time and for a few years after there was plenty in Ireland and that plenty was used lavishly. Milk, meat, strong-flavoured butter, and boiled ox-blood—these were staple foods and reared big-boned men and handsome women.

At the end of eating the old man went fumbling in a corner and came back with a cow's horn full of a pale liquid. He proffered it to me. " There is no harm in it," he told me. " 'Tis mild and old."

It was usquebaugh flavoured with wild honey, and, though old, it had retained the fire of youth. It made throat and eye smart, but I took my share manfully as required by ritual, and the old fellow left a bare mouthful at the bottom for the crone.

We went outside after food. The Gael bears ill with indoors while the sun is above ground, and that is why his dwelling is no more than a makeshift against night and weather. He is a tent-dweller, forced in this grey north to burrow in a clay bothy shaped not unlike a tent.

Now that I had broken bread, what men there were came out into the open. They were mostly old, and, after their habit, strolled to hear what news was going where my host and I leant on the wall of the pasture. And talk went back and forth.

" While the truce lasts," I told them, " I am paying a visit to my cousin, O'Cahan of Dungiven."

" Ay ! I thought you had the northern Gaelic," said my host. " A namely clan. 'Tis said young Donal Ballagh led three hundred gallowglasses at Clontibret."

" The slow road you are taking," put in another ancient who had a sharp-set tongue.

" It suits me well." I looked at my old host. " What road would you take yourself ? "

" Well now,"—he rubbed his chin—" 'tis like enough I would take the road yourself is on—if I was wanting to see a sept of O'Neill and he a friend of mine. Here now you are on the height of ground and only small streams to cross, and straight north from here are small townships of O'Duffys and O'Nuallans, who would be for hurting no one and he rightly inclined. That's the road till you cross the Blackwater into O'Neill's country, where no one at all troubles a stranger who would be a cousin of O'Cahan."

And that is the road I took, taking my time to it. I rode circumspectly and was careful of my little mare, and made acquaintance with the people of the soil. I ate with them,

slept with them, held converse with them, and found them
kin to the marrow of their bones. No man did me hurt or
sought to do so, for I was one of their own, passing through
on his own business and taking, as a matter of course, the
share that was due to him. I met no English soldier on that
road. The power of the English Queen did not reach in there.
Indeed it did not touch me until I had crossed the Blackwater
and thought myself safe in O'Neill's country.

I crossed the Blackwater within a mile of the mud fort of
Portmore, at that time held precariously for the Queen by
one Captain Williams, a tough-grained man of Wales. I
gave Benmee rein across the open, the first she had got since
Liffey side, and she stretched herself out at her gallantest
pace. In a matter of ten minutes we were into a scattered plantation of pine and out of it again on a rolling dry heathland.

Now I was surely safe in Ulster, with Dungannon the
stronghold of O'Neill scarcely a day's ride away. I drew
Benmee down to a walk, rode in between two round knolls,
ambled round a curve—and there, not more than a hundred
paces away, were two horsemen riding towards me !

I pulled Benmee in so sharply that she swerved half round,
and then the horsemen saw me and came spurring. With a
sudden beat of heart I recognised them. They were Sir
Francis Vaughan and his man Pybus. The right thing to
have done then was to go galloping back round the curve
and take to slanting northwards when I had the chance.
Benmee had it in her to show clean heels to the big English
horses, and there was no sense in risking capture so near safety.
Yet some dour spirit held me there, some deep-down distaste
of turning my back on this Englishman of mettle, who was
never unfair and for whom I had a respect. So I squared
Benmee round to them and waited. All I could do was to
throw back my long cloak, so that Vaughan could see I
carried a long sword but had not yet touched hilt of it. They
pulled up before me at honest distance, Pybus behind his
master.

" Well met," cried Vaughan pleasantly. " You have been long on the road."

" Thanks to you, Sir Francis Vaughan," I gave back.

He laughed. " I ask your pardon. Three thickpates make a poor compliment, and I am sorry you did not cut the thickest off at the neck."

I saw Tom Pybus grin, an honest and faithful man ; and in memory of that day by the Liffey ford he kept his beast tight-reined with one hand and held the other across his waist, close to his hilt. He rode a wide Flanders horse, and on the crupper of the saddle before him was strapped a hawking-frame, whereon were perched a brace of goshawks* hooded and tasselled. Sir Francis himself carried a gerfalcon on his gauntleted wrist and wore the green hawking-tunic and plumed cap of the cult. His only weapon was a light rapier a-swing at thigh, while Pybus wore his trooper's clumsy blade. All this I took in of instinct, and at the same time made sure that no other riders were in the reach of valley behind them. This meeting, then, was a chance one and my luck might hold.

" Are you not on the wrong side of the Blackwater, Master Gordon ? " Vaughan inquired banteringly, yet bitingly.

" And you, too, Sir Francis ? "

" No ! My Queen owns all this Ireland. In her name might I invite you back to Portmore ? "

He was making play with me now, and the Gael in me did not like it.

" I am on my way to visit cousins of mine up north," said I, " and I would like them to be with me when I visit you at Portmore."

" How many ? " asked he with understanding.

" A thousand," said I, " and maybe one or two more."

" One or two too many," he said and laughed ; and then he grew serious and his eye firmed on mine. " So you

* Kinds of large, short-winged hawk.

have made your choice at last—or was it your choice from the beginning ? "

" No," said I. " I had made no choice until your friend Captain Cosby—— "

" No friend of mine," he stopped me quickly. " Perdition to him ! "

There was silence then. This soldier and courtier was never so slow of speech. I think that he was perplexed, for his eyes frowned and his hand came up and stroked the hooded head of his falcon. Somehow he had a feeling for me, and it did not suit well with his loyalty to his Queen. Myself was growing restless inside. . I was too near Portmore, and two of the enemy were more than enough. At last he lifted his head.

" David Gordon," said he seriously, " will you keep a truce with me ? "

" Gladly."

" Go your road, then, but plight me your honour that you will say no word of what you have seen or heard at Bristol or Dublin."

I did not take two breaths to consider that.

" No," I said, " I will not pledge honour to that."

" Then you are finally against my Queen." His voice hardened. " And I must ask you to come back with me to Portmore."

" Your reason is a poor one—— "

" The reason of two against one ! You have no choice, and I do not want to draw sword on you."

" I know that," said I, " but here is your excuse for you."

And there was the blue-gleaming shine of my sword as it took the sun and the small keen tone of its song.

Vaughan was a quicker man than his servant. The gerfalcon fluttered down on the heather, and the rapier was out as soon as the Ferrara.

" This is folly," I said, in a final effort to be pacific. " Let us go our own roads."

For answer he drove his big charger at me his light weapon
at point. Now, a rapier on horseback is a childish weapon
against even a raw swordsman with a Ferrara blade. He had
to get home with his first thrust or have his guard smashed
through. Pybus was still tugging out his stiff blade as Vaughan
came in, lunging cleanly like a swordsman. I swerved handy
Benmee aside with a knee, and as he recovered his blade,
shore it clean off at the hilt. And there was Sir Francis
Vaughan reining back his horse and my point at his throat,
and his eyes steeled for the prick. But I recovered blade to
the salute, and— " Look to yourself ! " he warned.

Pybus was coming down on me with intent to kill, his
teeth bare, fury in his eyes—and dismay, too, for he thought
his master already dead. He launched the full swing of his
blade at me, a terrific head-smashing blow. But I saw it
coming from away behind his shoulder and glanced it carefully over my bonnet feather, and as he went past, bent flat
over empty hawking-frame by his own violence, I gave him
his deserts. I used the flat as I had at Liffey ford, but let him
have the full weight of it across buff shoulders so that he fell
on his horse's neck, and the next bound of the beast somersaulted him into the heather.

And then I did what I should have done in the beginning.
I gave Benmee her head, and we went full speed northward
up the curve of the valley. At the turn I swung in the saddle
for a look. Pybus, at a stout trot, was trundling away after
his mount, and Vaughan sat still in his saddle and looked after
me. I lifted my sword to him, and he threw up his broken
blade in a gesture of farewell and salutation. A gallant man
of the English.

CHAPTER VIII

IN THE STRONGHOLD OF THE O'NEILL

HERE at last was Dungannon, the hub of the northern power, and it was not even a walled town. O'Neill himself had burned it down the previous year as a drastic measure against the sudden advance of the English from Dundalk, that advance which had ended at stark Clontibret field. And now there was the big stone keep with its great walled bailey* and, so far as I could see, not another stone building in the place. It was a wide-scattered disarray of clay, wattled, and wooden houses. Some of the houses had gardens, some were enclosed by an earthen rampart, some hedged with the white-thorn in full bloom, and other lowly ones clustered in a close with a post-gate† at the end. Many of the wooden buildings were commodious and well-constructed, with steep-pitched roofs, stone chimneys, carved doorways, and walls painted in bright colours.

There was no regular street or paved way in the town. Here a width of as much as fifty paces lay between the houses, and there two gable-ends left scant room for a couple of horsemen abreast. Luckily the weather had been dry, and the clay road, packed hard, made easy going. There were dogs everywhere, big wolfhounds, lighter greyhounds, and a squat blue-grey beast of the otter-hound breed—and all of them that were in sight came barking at me in no unfriendly spirit.

I was taken with Dungannon. It was sunny and airy, more a camp than a town ; for, though women looked at me over cut-down doors and children pranked in the open, there were soldiers everywhere. Many of the large wooden houses within their raths served as barracks, and big clean-faced fighting-men moved about here and there in the lazy

* Inner defensive court.   † Postern, back-door, side entrance.

good-natured way of their class. Within one rath I saw the bonnets and kilts of Highlandmen, and was half-tempted to turn back to the unbarred gate, but when I looked into the next rath there were more and still more of my countrymen. So I rode on. I did not know then that O'Neill's *bonnachts** — his regular troops—were many of them mercenary soldiers from the Western Highlands.

I made my very best show that day. I had groomed Benmee, plaited her mane, flossed out her flowing tail; of her I need not be ashamed. I had ridden her judiciously all the way from Dublin, and now she was in sleeky hard condition, carrying her head and mincing her steps in this strange town like the vain little lady she was. Myself had shaved freshly that morning over a still pool, tried to smooth down the back wave of sullen red hair, re-set my blackcock's tail plume, and now I rode back straight and head up, my thrown-back cloak showing its lining of smooth fur and the polished hilt of Andrea Ferrara winking in the sun.

I moved along slowly, Benmee's neck arched to the rein, and though my head was still my eyes roved. The thought in my mind was that it must be eleven of the clock and near time for dinner, and that this was not Ireland if someone did not offer it to me. Better leave it to chance and keep trending towards the dún of O'Neill. Even now from that direction the odour of cooking meat came to me and made mouth water.

Many men saluted me frankly as we passed ; all of them looked knowingly at the clean legs of the mare ; no man at all hindered or questioned me. This was a free town. And then, as I opened the wide space before the dún, I overtook two men strolling easily, and they moved aside to let me pass. I drew in Benmee and lifted a hand, half in salute and half in query.

One of them sported a bonnet the marrow of my own, but instead of kilt he wore horseman-buff with a black

* Hired soldiers.

steel back-and-breast. A lantern-jawed man he was, with a long Scots nose. The other was a slim, supple young fellow with no covering on his notable yellow mane of hair. His short cloak was lined with rose-hued silk, and there were red selvedges to his bleached-linen tunic ; a gallant lad with a reckless blue eye and a smile about his mouth.

"Ho, man o' Scotland !" said the lantern-jawed man in clipped Gaelic of Strathclyde. "What clan ?"

"Gordon," I told him.

"So ! Mary Stuart's Highland hawks ! Not many of them stray this road. I am a Crawford out of Carrick-Kennedy country."

The young Irishman was running his eye over me and over Benmee. "Man, Hugh !" he cried. "Do they breed darlings like that mare in the Antrim glens ?" He looked at me with query in his eyes.

"They do not," said I.

"Maybe in Clandeboye ?"

"If you want to know, I come from Dublin," and I grinned to his gay smile.

"Dublin !" exclaimed Hugh Crawford the Scot, interest alight in his eye. "With message for O'Neill from the new Lord Deputy ?"

"I am on my way to visit O'Cahan of Dungiven. Is he by any chance in this place ?"

"Donal Ballagh ?" cried the Irishman. "He is not here—nor at Dungiven. Do you not know ? He is truce hostage with Bingham in Galway."

And there was my luck gone awry. This custom of hostage was usual in Irish truces. In the present one with the English the Ulster leaders had yielded as hostages six young chiefs of note.

"Galway !" I repeated the word after him.

"Ay, Galway ! sixty leagues from here, and there he will be—having the fine times—while the truce lasts."

I was once again thinking bitterly of Dame Luck. All

the way from Dublin—all the way from Arras—had I come
to see this cousin O'Cahan, and he was beyond reach at the
other side of Ireland. Blood is thicker than water, and the
family tie is a close one amongst us. I had looked forward to
offering my services to a chief of my own blood, knowing
that he would be understanding with my shortcomings.
Now I was only a stranger amongst strangers—one Scots
fighting-man among the many—and tall as I was and strong
as I was, I had not much to offer ; a bloodless sword, a sour
experience of life, and no experience at all of war. Very well,
then !

I heard the young Irishman speaking. " Do not be minding
that at dinner-time," he said lightly. " Come and eat with us,
man of the Gordons."

Already I was beginning to feel aloof with my native
dourness. " Let me not trouble you. The Ordinary*—— "

He laughed. " There is none. No man goes hungry in
the dún of O'Neill. My name is Doncadh Donn Maguire."

Here then was one of O'Neill's young smiters, son of
that great Maguire who had scattered the English at the Ford-
of-Biscuits.†

" Come on, lad ! " said Crawford. " The O'Neill keeps
open table."

No doubt this tough and hard-headed Scots leader of
mercenaries had been deciding in his own mind that a man
who was come out of Dublin was worth questioning, and that
the man to do the questioning was not far away.

" Thank you," said I then. " My name is David Gordon."

I slid off my saddle-pad, slung rein over arm, and the
three of us walked across the wide exercise-ground towards
the great keep. It was as stirring as a hive, this dún of O'Neill.
Outside the big bailey were a score or more of Irish-bred
ponies in care of ragged horse-boys, and Maguire called one

* Public dinner at an inn.

† At Enniskillen, where an English force was routed by O'Donnell
with the loss of a supply train of provisions.

of these to take charge of Benmee. We entered the bailey through a postern-gate in the rear wall, and found a multitude like a clan gathering—chiefs and retainers in full custume. Surely, O'Neill kept open house.

Hugh O'Neill had been gently bred and nurtured, and this courtyard showed it. There was a great square of closely cut green lawn in the middle and beds of tulips flamed along the edges. Beyond rose the massive bulk of the keep, with an open door at the head of cut-stone steps, a black arch piercing the middle, and tall glazed windows looking inwards. Along the sunny side of the bailey was a wide terrace under a light pent-roof, and in there scullions were busy laying immensely long tables. Groups of men lolled about in the grass, waiting for the dinner-hour ; clan chiefs in their white and saffron tunics and silk-lined cloaks ; gallowglass captains in steel and buff ; young men, bare-headed and clean-shaven ; old men with long hair and beards ; shanachies, harpers, brehons—all the retainers of a royal Gaelic Court. And there were ladies there too, tight-bodiced, flowing-kirtled, with lace and linen on their plaited hair.

Near mid-green was a large group round a garden-bench, whereon sat a man and two or three ladies.

" That is O'Neill taking his ease," Doncadh Donn Maguire informed me.

I was too far away to note more than that he was a man with a beard trained in the English mode.

Crawford murmured that he had a word to say to the chief, and hurried across the lawn. He looked back significantly at Maguire, and that lad, with a comradely freedom, put his hand within my arm and slanted me towards the dining-terrace.

" These fellows will be talking, dry as an old dyke— and keeping dinner late. You will be sorry missing Donal Ballagh ? "

" I am."

" Thick as thieves we are—I never heard him speak of you."

" You would not."

" You know him well ? "

" I do not know him at all."

We looked at each other and burst out laughing.

" *Mhuire !* " he exclaimed. " You would be a good man to tell a secret to—and bury it safe. Ah ! there's old Paud going to blow the cowhorn."

That dinner of O'Neill's was an informal plenteous affair. As soon as the dinner-horn winded, the multitude drifted easily towards the tables. There was no order, nor was there any hurry. The crowd circled round, found places, and set to work. The top cross-table was reserved for O'Neill, the ladies, and any of his older chiefs who might be visiting ; that table was covered with damask and laid with plate, Dutch pottery, and Venetian glass ; there were forks for the ladies and finger bowls for whoever cared to use them. The other tables were of bare planed oak and furnished with beechen platters and methers, and drinking-horns edged with silver. Maguire bestowed me amongst fellows of his own at a table about half-way down, and it was surely the noisiest table there.

As I have said, the Irish were notable meat-eaters, and here was meat for any army ; beef and pork, fowl and game, venison from the woods, salmon and eels out of Bann river, and for the first time since leaving Dublin I tasted wheaten bread. The drink was even more plenteous than the meats ; usequebaugh, mead and metheglin,* a new English beer, Spanish wine in jars, and Garonne wine in flasks, and never a mug of water. And everyone ate hugely and drank copiously, and made talk and laughter without end—not like the forthright Saxon who centres his mind on his meat, nor like the French who are also gay talkers, but use extravagant gesture with knife and chicken-bone. And, above the noise

* A kind of mead, made chiefly from honey.

and clatter, came the skirl of the pipes from where two tall
fellows strutted back and forth on the gravel outside O'Neill's
table and played ports* that I had heard in far Glenfiddich.

Some time towards the end of the dinner Maguire left my
side, and returned in a matter of a couple of minutes. He
placed his hand on my shoulder. " O'Neill would like a word
—would like to make your acquaintance, David Gordon,"
he said.

I had been expecting that message.

CHAPTER IX

THE PLAN OF CAMPAIGN

I STOOD before O'Neill with his household and his chiefs,
and I bowed to him and to the ladies. The one sitting by
him was young and lovely, brown-haired and soft-eyed, and
I felt big and awkward and ugly.

" Hugh," said Doncadh Donn Maguire familiarly, " this
is David Gordon out of Alban, riding up from Dublin to see
Donal Ballagh O'Cahan."

There was but small formality in Gaeldom, where there
was vast pride in race. Hugh O'Neill was a queen's
earl, but he was not feudal lord. He was chief of the clan—
father, brother, friend—to be addressed frankly and called
by his name : Hugh, Hugh O'Neill ; but if one was called
upon to be formal one used the proudest title that could be
yielded—O'Neill.

He rose to his feet to me. " Gordon ! " said he, and his
voice rolled the word deeply. " To be sure. You are Donal
Ballagh's cousin ? "

And I again bowed.

" I knew it. I saw your father in this very dún when I

* Tunes.

was a boy. You are welcome to Dungannon, David Gordon. You are my cousin too—twice removed."

His hand clasped mine firmly, and his eyes met mine so keenly that I felt the shock of their scrutiny. Blue eyes they were, deep-set and close-set under brows, and they had a shock like ice or fire. He was a man of middle height, this great O'Neill, with good shoulders, notably long arms, and the slightly bowed legs of the horseman. He wore a silken tunic like his chiefs, went bareheaded like them ; but, unlike them, he carried a trained spade-beard on his chin—a fair red beard, already flecked with grey.

He turned to the lovely brown-haired woman. " Woman-of-the-house," said he, " this is our kinsman David Gordon. His father Iain, a black gerfalcon, stole my cousin Nuala O'Cahan, from under her father's nose and off to Scotland with her."

The lady smiled to my salutation. " 'Tis a bad habit men have," she said aptly and drew brisk laughter, for she herself had been stolen by O'Neill from under the nose of her brother, the Marshal Henry Bagenal.

" My word ! " exclaimed Hugh Crawford, sitting across the table. " Do you never forget anything you ever saw or heard, O'Neill ? "

" But that was a great exploit, Hugh, and she, Nuala—God rest her—the heart-breaker of the north.—And how is Iain Gordon standing the years, David ? "

" He is dead, O'Neill," said I, speaking for the first time.

" God rest him ! It is good to see one's kin in loneliness." He glanced at young Maguire. " Does David Gordon know about O'Cahan ? "

" Hostage in Galway—— "

" But not for long, I am thinking." He looked at me and smiled—a wonderfully taking smile, coming out from below his stern eyes, that made me understand why men and women liked him. " You will be welcome at Dungiven, I think—

and you are welcome at Dungannon, I know. It is not forgotten that your father was on O'Neill's side that bad day in
Antrim."

" And now," cried his lady, " you will be talking old times
and old fights, and we will leave you to it."

The ladies left us, the pipers stopped playing, and hurried
to their meat, and O'Neill took my arm. " Sit down," he
said. " Crawford you know. This is Maguire of Fermanagh,
who has not dowered a certain lad with much sense—— "

" True for you, Hugh," agreed Donn Maguire's father,
a stern man with a white beard.

O'Neill sat me down by himself. " A pleasant ride from
Dublin you would have ? " he said carelessly.

" Very pleasant, O'Neill," I replied.

" It is sometimes not easy these days to reach Dungannon
from Dublin—but of course you would have a safe-conduct
from the new Lord Deputy ? "

Here was the deft half-query, the first of many that would
winnow my news like corn from chaff. And I felt rise in me
that strange national dourness that ever sullenly sets itself
against winnowing. The men about me were silent, waiting
for my answer ; but instead of answering I put a half-question
of my own.

" There was a friend of your cause, O'Neill, on the borders
of the Pale—Colum O'More ? "

" He and his clan."

" He is dead."

" Dead ! Colum O'More dead ? "

" Slain in Dublin by an English officer."

" What dog did it ? " It was Donn Maguire cried that.

" One Captain Cosby of Cong."

" Cosby the Killer ! They say he wears a mail shirt in his
sleep."

O'More had been one of O'Neill's trusted chiefs. The
word of his death was a shock to everyone who heard—
except, it might be, to O'Neill himself. O'Neill had too

much on his mind to be shocked by the death of one man, and in his time had helped to slay Irish chiefs to foster his single cause. " The man who killed O'More," he said quietly, " did disservice to his Queen. With Offaly and the Glens roused, Dublin will need a full garrison.—Well, David Gordon ? "

" I was friendly with O'More," I went on. " I had to flee from Dublin—— "

" You are safe from the Queen's men here," said O'Neill, a small touch of pride in his voice.

But that word " safe " nettled me. " I did not come for safety," I said, I fear ungraciously, " but to offer my services to my cousin."

" I am your cousin, too, David Gordon," said O'Neill gently.

" I have little to offer you, O'Neill," I said glumly.

" Well said, Scot ! " cried Crawford. " That is the hilt of an Andrea Ferrara you have there, and besides being a sword it is a good one."

" Look ! " I cried then, so that I must be understood. " I had Cosby open to a plain lunge above the gorget, and I missed by three fingers. That is the kind of swordsman I am." Let me say now that the missing of that lunge had rankled in me. If my father had been alive he would never have forgiven me bungling that plain thrust.

O'Neill put his hand on my shoulder. " Swording is only an art," he said. " It is the man I look for."

" For what I am worth," I blurted out, glad to get it over.

His hand pressed. " You are mine," he said. " Leave it to me. Come out now in the sunlight—these boys are getting noisy."

Many of his following were still at table, and the young ones were beginning to lift voices in song. O'Neill, Maguire, Crawford and I went out on the grass.

We sat down on the garden bench, and O'Neill was no longer indirect in his questioning. " What is your news out of Dublin, Cousin David ? "

I knew what he meant. " De Burgh has brought reinforcements of five thousand men with culverin and mangonels,"
I told him.

" A pleasant peace-time force ! " said old Maguire dryly.

O'Neill's eyes darkened and deepened. " What quality ? "
he asked me.

" Three thousand veteran troops and two thousand from
the southern train-bands."

" The veterans are as good as the best," said Crawford
judiciously, " but the youngsters do not like cold steel."

" Cold steel is better than hot lead from top of a wall,
with a hard Scots head safe behind the same wall," said
Maguire with stern humour. This was a half-jibe at Crawford,
who was noted for the art he had acquired in the French wars
of defending dúns.

O'Neill took no notice. His eyes were on mine.

" I was only eight days in Dublin," I replied to that waiting
look, " but already the train-bands were being drafted into
the southern garrisons."

" And the veterans held in Dublin ? "

" For the time. And the day before I left, de Burgh had a
Council with his Connacht leaders."

" The Connacht leaders ! The full leash ! I thank you
cousin. You have already served me well."

" You may thank a dead man, O'Neill."

We were silent for a space, and O'Neill in a muse of his
own. He lifted his head at last and looked at Crawford, his
eyes crinkling. " What would you do, Hugh, if you were the
English Lord Deputy ? "

" God forgive us, O'Neill, but I would do something."

" The direct thing."

" Ay so ! If I had five thousand reinforcements I would
come straight at you and make you burn Dungannon a second
time."

" And we would be giving you Clontibret over again—
you blood-thirsty loyalist," said Maguire.

" What would yourself do, Maguire ? "

" I would be thinking it out to myself," said Maguire cannily. " But I know what Hugh O'Neill would be doing if he were in de Burgh's place."

" Go on, Prince of Ulster," mocked Crawford.

" He would wait till harvest, when the clans are scattered in field and shieling, come down full force through the Gap-of-the-North, and put all Ulster under fire and sword."

" Surely," agreed O'Neill, " that is the wise plan. But note that Conyers Clifford in Connacht is also eager to come down on us through the western gap at Bellashanny."*

" And Hugh Roe O'Donnell, my darling, will be saying a word or two to that," said Maguire with satisfaction.

" With his clan at the harvest ? No." O'Neill turned to Crawford. " Hugh, we will put you behind a stone wall. I am going to lend you to O'Donnell—you and your Scots— with word that you are to garrison Bellashanny and the fords of Samhaoir† while the clans are in shieling. We shall be attacked on two fronts, as I see it, and if you lose Bellashanny you will let Clifford in on my rear."

" I will not let him if I can stop him," said Crawford mildly.

And then O'Neill turned to me. " I have work for you too, David Gordon. You are now sept to O'Neill, and O'Neill will have to bear the brunt of the coming fight. Your cousin Donal Ballagh is in Galway, and his foster-brother Calvagh MacManus holds Dungiven. There you will go with a written word from me. With Calvagh you will warn the clan and help to lead it when the onset comes." He slapped me on the shoulder. " And that is enough for one day. We will go to the ladies now and hear the harpers play.— Come brothers ! "

Thus it was that the great O'Neill gave me work to do.

---

* Ballyshannon.   † Ancient name for river Erne.

CHAPTER X

THE DÚN OF THE O'CAHAN

THERE now was the O'Cahan stronghold of Dungiven standing above the shallow clear waters of the Roe, and there was I, David Gordon, riding down to it, two days out of Dungannon, and the high moors behind me.

I had stayed the best part of a week in O'Neill's camp and had learned to value the force and prudence of the great leader ; and despite myself I had become friendly with young Doncadh Donn Maguire. He had accompanied me on my road as far as the head of Cairntogher Pass. He would have come all the way to Dungiven if O'Neill had not strictly warned him that he must be back among his own clan in three days, and that warning he dared not disobey.

A sunny afternoon at the end of May, as I drew rein at the margin of the Roe and looked across at the dún. Everything was quiet and still ! The blackbird's song was done and the thrush not ready for his evening trill, and there came to my ears only the soft and lonely murmur of the river—a small, apart, uncanny, quiet chuckle at something not human. It put a weight of childish loneliness on me and held me there in a thoughtless sort of gloom based outside all life.

Up a long paved causeway beyond the ford was the grey-stone squat battlemented tower of the dún ; a wing of wall ran either side of it with a guard tower at each end, and it was pierced in the middle by an arch opening into darkness. The slope right and left of the causeway was of worn grass and clear of all habitation, but round the side of the northern corner-tower was a scattering of wooden and clay bothies— a whole hamlet. And then I heard children laugh, and my eyes followed the course of the stream to where a clan of them were wading knee-deep in the clear water, intent on a pursuit

of eels under the flat slabs of mossy stone—a game I knew.
It was a quiet and happy scene, and the gloom was only in myself.

And now I set Benmee at the ford and splashed across
at a walk, and at a walk rode quietly up the causeway, throwing back my cloak to show my sword in sheath and no weapon
in hand.

Two lengths away I checked Benmee, and a kern, a lean
lathy lad, stepped in front of the arch. " Where your road,
friend ? " he inquired in friendly enough fashion.

" Calvagh MacManus with word from O'Neill."

" God save him ! Calvagh MacManus ? So—so ! O'Neill
would not be hearing the news yet. You are welcome, tall
hero. Calvagh is within the court. I will take your horse."

He yelled in through the arch, and another kern came
tumbling out of a side passage to help him.

I walked in under the gloom of the arch and came out
into the full sunlight of the bailey. It was not more than
half the size of O'Neill's great one, and a glance showed
that there was no wife or woman in this household. It was
the stronghold of single men and soldiers. Penthouse buildings
of weathered wood ran round three sides ; one-half of it was
paved with cobbles, the other was packed clay. In the middle
was a big high-pitched building with walls of heavy oak, roof
of rye thatch, and wide unglazed window openings ; and
frames of windows and open door were intricately carved in
scroll-work and coloured red ochre ; here and there in
corners grass and weeds grew undisturbed.

Before this middle-house on the packed earth two
young men were engaged in a putting contest with a smooth
round stone, big as a child's head. One was a middle-sized
powerful red-headed figure. The other was tall—very tall—
and in a short-sleeved linen tunic. Nearly a score of men
were looking on, and an old white-haired long-bearded
fellow was holding forth, while a black Austin friar made
fun of him.

I walked slowly—and something stiffly after my long

ride—towards them, my cloak thrown back on my shoulders.
The tall young fellow was balancing for the putt, and, all
eyes being fixed on him, none saw me. With smooth and
easy power he pivoted from foot to foot, and the stone went
sailing in a huge curve.

" Ho ! Ho ! Ho ! laughed the friar happily. " Beat
that, if beating is in you, Calvagh son of Manus."

The old white-beard lifted his voice—a most surprising
volume of a voice. " A good cast—good enough ! But
the full spade short of his father's best—God rest him ! "

" Ho ! Ho ! Ho ! " the priest again laughed. " Was
there ever a son to beat his father ? "

The tall lad strode across and playfully shook a clenched
hand in the old fellow's beard. " You big bellowing old
shield-striker ! " he cried. " Two years ago you said the
same thing of a cast a full spade short of that one."

The old fellow grinned unashamed and opened his mouth
for retort—and thereupon his eyes fixed themselves on me.
And there they widened and his mouth was no wider. Then
he blinked rapidly, gathered his look close on me and hurriedly
crossed himself. " God be praised ! " he half whispered,
and even his half-whisper had volume. " Your father come
back to life in all his might ! "

The tall young man turned quickly, and we looked at
each other. Who he was I did not guess, but I knew that
he was not Calvagh MacManus. The broad red man was
MacManus. This was no common man, I knew, but if his
hair had been red-gold I might have taken him for the famous
O'Donnell, ally of O'Neill. I think that this young man there
was the bonniest man I ever saw—I have ever seen. He was
tall and supple like a spear, with a mass of black curls over a
white square of brow ; his face had a healthy pallor, and his
keen dark-blue eyes were well set under black brows—a keen
lean face with a fine salty humour to it. There and then he
set alight in me that spark of liking that must come at the
first glance or not at all.

We stood there a few strides apart and looked at each
other, and all the others were still, too, except white-poll,
who had his hand tugging in his beard. The young chief
made the first move. He came at me slowly, but directly,
and placed his two hands gently down on my shoulders—
and our eyes were level. " I know you," he said. " You
are my cousin David Gordon, out of Scotland."

" But—— "

" I am Donal Ballagh O'Cahan."

" But—— "

" I know. I got back from Galway yesterday." His eyes
crinkled. " And the devil never came faster ! "

" I am David Gordon," said I then. " I am from Arras
in Picardy to see you—cousin."

His hands pressed my shoulders. " You are welcome
a thousand times." A little glow came behind his eyes and
I knew that I was welcome.

For the first time in my life I felt that I was welcome
for myself—a lump came up to my throat and I could not
help my eyebrows twitching.

The white-beard shanachie was at my cousin's shoulder.
" I knew—I knew first," his great voice proclaimed. " He
is the dead spit of your father when he was young."

" God forbid ! " said I, swallowing the lump. " He was
not the ugliest man in Ulster ! "

" He was that," the old fellow boomed, " and the best
man at your right hand or at your left in the same place—
and the best caster of the heavy stone."

Donal Ballagh saw that I was touched. He swung round
to my side, his hand on my arm. " This young fellow of
four score or five," he presented, " is one Turlough son of
Teaclan, and once on a time he used to sing a lay and pluck
a harp string—and thinks he can do both yet. And this is
Father Senan of the Priory, who says our prayers for us."

The priest came forward. He was well past middle years
but sturdy, and there was not a grey hair in his strong brown

beard. He wore the black frock of the Austin friars, and his hair was close cut in the Celtic tonsure from ear to ear. " I knew your father, David Gordon," he said. " This old fellow Turlough—he was not so old then—the two of us rowed the young pair over Bann river the night they went from here." His blue-grey eyes searched me with a wistful look. " Is there anything of Nuala O'Cahan in you ? "

" No," I said. " She was gentle and beautiful " ; and I smiled to his look.

His eyes filled and his mouth quivered. " Ah ! " he cried, " there she is—there she is now, deep down in you. Do I not remember her, when she smiled ? Your father—is he well ? "

" He is dead," I told him.

" His soul with God—and with her ! "

" Amen," said Donal softly. " We are in like case, cousin." Then he lifted his voice. " Here, Calvagh—Calvagh Mac-Manus my foster-brother, who by his easy ways in this dún has put a month's work before me to thin the paunches of these fellows you see grinning."

The garrison gallowglasses laughed, and in that laughter was the admiring confident note that showed that this strong-hold was a happy place for men. MacManus had pulled his tunic over his head, and he came and took my hand with a murmured word of welcome. He had a square face and a grim one for a man so young, and all feeling was now hid behind a grey eye. In after days, when we grew to know each other, he told me that he was filled with a passion of jealousy that first hour. That I can understand, knowing the closeness of the foster-tie.

My cousin was considerate of me to the end. He drew me towards the door of the mid-house. " A long road behind you, my light ! You will have a bite now and a sup, and we with you. Time enough for talk. Come, brothers ! "

And so I was made welcome to Dungiven.

The inside of the mid-house was one great high room. It had a stone chimney, a bare floor of hewn boards, a long

oaken table on trestles, a scatter of straw-bottomed chairs
and backless benches, and all round it were uncurtained
alcoves wherein were wooden sleeping-benches. It was, in
fact, the living-room of the dún, whose cold stone chambers
were mostly used for stores and armaments. The Gael never
could bide in a dungeon of stone.

In there they plied me with cold venison, barley-meal
bread, and *coirm*,* and joined me at the eating—Donal,
Calvagh, Turlough, and the friar. They talked and presently
I found myself talking too, giving a lame enough account of
France, my father's death, and my journey as far as Dungannon. When I got myself as far as that place, I remembered
for the first time that day that I had a written message from
O'Neill. I fished it from my satchel—a folded scrap of vellum
with the Red Hand of O'Neill stamped on a splash of wax.

Donal Ballagh looked at the name on the outside and
flicked it across to Calvagh MacManus, who looked over
the writing and handed it back, and Donal read the formal
Gaelic aloud.

*Calvagh MacManus, friend. David Gordon bears this, cousin
in the first degree to O'Cahan, and my kinsman as well as in my
service.*—" Ah, ha ! Red Earl—not servant but sept."—
He is a swordsman of skill—" Not so ! " said I, " but a bungler."
—*But he lacks experience of war. I bestow him in your command.*—
" The wise fox he is."—*Take heed now. The truce with the
Sassenach they will break at the harvest time, and they will strike in
on our front and on O'Donnell's front, I think. It will be hard fighting
and our lack will be trained horse. I look to the O'Cahan clan for a
mounted standard, and this my kinsman you will find useful to teach
sword-play against the coming of your chieftain and your brother. At
your service, O'Neill.*—" And that is that ! A wise letter.
Hugh knows."

Donal sat there staring at the scrap of vellum, and a
far-away look came in his eyes. " War in the harvest time,"
he murmured. " War—war—war ! June—July—August !

* A kind of ale.

three months—short enough and long enough—if word comes." He twisted the letter in his hands, still musing, and then suddenly threw off this introspection that had brought a touch of colour to his face. "Three months ! " he cried, " and we with our work before us.—I am glad that you are here, David."

" I am glad, too, Donal," said I.

CHAPTER XI

DAYS AT DUNGIVEN

I WAS happy at Dungiven, and a close tie grew between my cousin Donal and me. He told me some of the many things he had seen and done. He had been as far as Greenwich Court with O'Neill ; he had been to Lisbon and Cadiz in his uncle's ship out of Derry Columcille ; and though he was younger than I was, he had led his clan of a thousand able-bodied fighting-men in half a score of stark fights, notably at the Ford-of-Biscuits and Clontibret.

But there was one episode in his life that he could not be got to dwell on : the recent breaking of hostage at Galway. Every man—and every woman too—of the clan was curious to know the why and how of that business, but all he would say was that he had a private quarrel with Rickard the Sassenach, Baron of Dunkellin, and that Governor Bingham had taken sides with the loyalist and put Donal himself behind bars, thus breaking the terms of hostage ; whereupon Donal had broken prison and made his way home by secret roads he knew.

What the subject of the quarrel was no one in Dungiven was told ; but I for one could make a near guess. Often and often in the midst of talk I had watched Donal go into that spell of day-dreaming where the face smiles and grows

wistful. Doubtless others saw as much as I did, or more ;
but after the manner of the breed, no one dared say a word
till O'Cahan took it on himself to open the subject.

After ten days or a fortnight in Dungiven, Donal took
me on a round of visits to the scattered septs of his clan,
and made sure that I became accepted as one entitled to
all the rights of the blood. And as he progressed he arranged
for a gathering, at Dungiven, of his chiefs and captains.

There for three days, in the intervals of terrific hurling
matches and profuse feastings, were discussed the plans of
the clan for harvest and the campaign. The crops were to
be cut and lifted as they ripened, and the women and the
old must do more than their share of the harvesting. This
man and that and the other, by name and degree, had to
equip ten, twenty, forty gallowglasses and so many kern
and hold them ready for the hosting. Such and such a one
could mount three or six or ten horsemen. " When—now ?
Next week ! Fine, surely ! Send them down to the dún,
horse and man. Horse are needed and horse take time to
train." So it was that in a short time we had a squadron of
fifty horse at Dungiven and lively times with them. Donal,
Calvagh, and I spent hours marshalling and drilling, and with
a new enthusiasm I set about teaching sword-play on horseback ; how to avoid the arm-wrench of the full lunge, how to
draw the too-eager first swing and follow the parry with a
deadly backhand cut, how to make sure that though your
man overrode you, you left empty saddle behind.

There was one man in Dungiven who, I think, loved
me better than he loved his chief. That man was Father
Senan the Austin friar. I was my mother's son and he fathered
me. He was a wise, kindly, sturdy old man and if he had any
fault it was an inordinate love of angling and a lack of patience
if anyone dared to dispute with him on that art. From
observation he had devised a new method, where his lure
imitated the natural fly that brings the fish clean out of
water in a bonny silver curve. He took charge of me from

the beginning ; he taught me to fish in his own fashion, extolled the virtue of a small fly with a woodcock wing and a moth body, of another grey-brown one for early June, and a red-brown one for treacherous August. With his quiet wisdom he set my feet on the road of understanding ; in the confessional he used to sit back and talk to me of things that had nothing to do with the shriving of sins, so that my friends twitted me on the grievous load that kept me so long on my knees ; and when I smiled, as was not now so infrequent, his bearded face would light up and then grow wistful, mindful of memories long ago.

So I was happy at Dungiven.

I come now to an evening in July. A fine clear evening with the faint hum of midges in the air, after a cloudy week of thundery showers.

Donal and I with Father Senan had spent the afternoon at the fishing down the full-flowing amber reaches of the Roe, and the fishing had been good. With a silver and blue hackled* lure tied for us by the old priest we had made spoil among a fresh run of salmon, round-girthed hen-fish up from northern sea.

Late in the evening, and hungry as hawks, we fared dunwards, our catch—at least a score—slung in panniers over the withers of a hill pony.

Ferdoragh the gate-ward came down to the ford to meet us. " A messenger here for you, Donal Ballagh O'Cahan," he shouted above the splash we made, the water up to our knees.

" From O'Neill ? " Donal inquired quickly.

" All the way from Galway," he says.

Donal checked in ankle-depth of water, checked dead-still for one draw of breath, and then stepped out on dry ground. " We will see him," he said, carefully quiet. He made no hurry. He said no word to us ; but Father Senan looked across at me behind him, frowned half-smilingly, and shook his tonsured head.

* Hook and fly dressed with feather.

The household was at supper when we got in, and the messenger from Galway was at home in that company. He was no townsman, but a big black-bearded fellow of the gallowglass caste, with the hugest pair of hands I had ever seen in a man. At the moment they were enveloping a wooden ale-piggin, and I did not see the piggin till he laid it down as he rose to his feet. " A writing for O'Cahan," he said, and fumbled in the breast of his rough crotal tunic.

" You are welcome, Teig Ironhand," greeted Donal gently.

The messenger tendered the folded missive. I saw that it was tied with a rose-red riband of silk from which hung a small seal.

Donal took the letter, read it quickly, and brought his eyes keenly to the man's face. " All well, Ironhand ? " he inquired with significance.

" Well, surely, my heart—and bell-metal for soundness."

Donal looked all round the room, and every man there of us had his eye somewhere else. He looked at me, and I was loosing the thongs of my wet footgear. I soon became aware that all the men knew as well as I what had weighed on our chief's mind.

He sat down quietly at my side and ate with me. But when old Turlough Mac an Teaclan ran his hand across the strings of his harp, and wistful lovely notes came about us, and deep true notes that made the heart stir—then Donal, head in hand, looked out of drugged eyes and forgot us all.

When supper was over, the half-dark was about us, and men moved quietly away so that in a short while we were alone, Donal and I. And after a time I got to my feet and went out alone and sadly under the moon and the thin stars, and as I walked I found Donal at my side. We paced up and down, as was our custom, but for long and long we said nothing.

Donal spoke first, after clearing his throat twice. " To-morrow," he said calmly, " I leave you in command."

" As you command, O'Cahan," said I formally.

" I will be away for a time."

I had no word to say to that and after a pause he went on.

" I am going down into Connacht—I suppose you know."

I had to help him. " I know you have a letter there," I blurted out, " twisting your heart-strings, and I know that it is the letter of a woman."

" Who will be my wife," he said softly.

" Oh, lucky woman ! " I cried in spite of me, a sombre weight on my heart. I was losing this lad that I loved.

" She is Amy Burke," he told me, " daughter of Rickard the Sassenach of Dunkellin."

" The man you quarrelled with ! "

" And she the cause. I met—my lady—at a reception of Bingham's in Galway, and after at Cashlean-na-Kirka on Upper Corrib, and at her home in Dunkellin—and otherwheres. We came to think alike—and knew it. We did nothing underhand. I spoke to her father, that long narrow man. He would have none of me for a son-in-law. He said so. He said it at great length. He is ten times more of the loyalist than the old dog-fox his father of Clanricard, and he gave me all his choice thoughts on us as rebel dogs of the North. What he said I would stand from no other man, and will not stand from him again. He is nothing to me or to Amy any more. That was in Galway. We decided to wed and say nothing till the hostage time expired—she decided as much as I did. Foolish we were, maybe ? "

" Maybe you were," said I.

" We failed anyway. A spy was about us somewhere. The dawn we were to be wed I slipped out of my quarters straight into the waiting arms of Bingham's guard, and five or ten minutes after that I was behind iron bars. Amy, as I learned later, was whisked off to Athlone under the wardship of the Governor, Sir Conyers Clifford. What was I to do ? "

" You came home."

"And broke prison and hostage at the same time. Not a hard task, either. No tight guard was kept on me. Teig Ironhand slung me a long *scian* through the bars a floor above ground—and my gaoler was not caring greatly for the point of it—so I walked out soft and easy, met Teig and had a talk with him, and got home here a day before yourself. And word came to-day, a letter from my lady herself, by the hand of Teig her foster-father." He touched the breast of his tunic. "As long as she was in Clifford's ward inside the walls of Athlone nothing could be done, but now she is back with her father in a strong place he has down beside the Clare border. But not for long ! Rickard does not trust me—or her. In ten days—a fortnight at most—he is taking her to Dublin and sending her from there to Greenwich Court in Ormonde's train. And she says, ' I am ready now, Donal. Will you come ? ' "

The pride in his voice stirred me. "My word ! " said I, "did she say that ? "

"Her very words. And to-morrow I go."

"Alone ? "

"Alone I would like to go, but alone I might miss the one chance. She is well guarded, and Dunkellin has a garrison of picked Sassenach in the place. I do hope to snatch her single-handed, but a sudden sally might be the only chance for us. I am taking ten of your horsemen—and Father Senan to wed us—the smallest force I dare trust for what may be needed."

"And Calvagh MacManus ? "

"No. I leave Calvagh with you."

"In that case I come with you. It would not be a nice thing to put me in command over your foster-brother." There was ever a small jealousy there.

Donal peered in my face. "Is that why you would come ? " he queried prickingly.

"Look ! " said I dourly. "Do you command me to stay ? "

" I do not."

" Then I come."

" Come, then, pighead," he cried at me, and shook me with both his hands. " Man, David, I am foolish to let you but I want you at my shoulder—in fight if fighting comes, and in peace when Senan speaks the words over my lady and me. You are my nearest kin—and nearest me, too—and second in Dungiven whatever befalls. David, the thing I am doing will make no difference between us two ? You know that ? "

" I know that," I lied stoutly.

CHAPTER XII

THE AMBUSH ON THE GALWAY ROAD

ALL through the night we had ridden hard and the horses were dead weary. Even my own hardy Benmee faltered now and then. They were weary although, before making this last long burst, we had given them a four hours' rest in a hazel clump well back from, and looking down, on the Galway road. The horses were spent because we had come all the long way from Dungiven at a breaking pace—down to the narrows of the Erne, where we had swum across into Breffni, round by Loch Gara through MacDermott and Costello country—and rough country at that—and so skirting the MacWilliam and MacTheobald lands, where at last we had to move warily. But luck had been with us all the road, and now, this fifth day, we were on the last long leg.

We had crossed the Galway road with the fall of night —a clear night with the moon near the full—and thereafter Teig Ironhand had led the way and in a hurry. That country south of the Galway road was flat and heavily wooded, and among the woods were spreads of dangerous marshes dark under the moon. But Teig knew his way. He kept trending westwards and still westwards under the curtain of the trees and, sometime before the lift of dark, came down to the margin of a wide plain, a waste of heather that whispered sadly under the dawn wind. There we halted and gave our horses breathing space.

In the break of dawn a black pine-ridge showed away in front, and in another quarter-hour we burst through a thick breast of sallies and came in amongst the trees. And there Teig halted and we gathered round him. " We are here now, O'Cahan," he said, pride in his voice. " This is Esker Riada, and beyond in the vale is the dún. There is no good in me any more till I put sleep over me."

" Nor in any of us," said Donal. " Rest it is."

We found a trickle of water amongst the sallies, and there in there we tethered the horses. Ourselves went into the brink of the Esker among the pines, where the ground was dry and sandy, with a fine mat of brown needles. There we lay down wearily. Our ration of provisions had run out in the night and I was very empty, but stronger than hunger was the desire to sleep, and sleep I did under my long cloak.

It was high day when Donal shook me awake out of a league-deep sleep. Teig bent over his shoulder and pointed to the ridge above.

" Come and see," whispered Donal, and the two turned and started to climb. Reaching the crown of the ridge, we lay down and looked out on as pleasant a scene as eyes ever saw after hard days.

We looked over the tops of trees on a green and pleasant vale, parkland clumped with orderly plantations, with here and there the brighter green of growing corn. In the middle distance a stream flowed and rippled, and my eyes followed its course westwards ; and there, not two miles away, was the lifting plane of the Atlantic sea, the green waters of Galway Bay brilliant under the sun. Southwards of it tall cliffs lifted shoulders out of the green, and the sun was swallowed in the black fronts of them.

Donal elbowed me, and I followed his pointing finger. "There it is, now." His voice was low and deep.

It was our goal, the stronghold of Dunkellin, a mile away eastwards. It stood on a knoll above the stream, a strong square tower with a high mantling wall, and below it near the water was the usual scattered hamlet and the Norman tower of a church.

As it happened, however, it was not at the dún that we were to find our quarry. From a herd-boy, a mat-haired barefooted kern named Ruari whom Teig had laid hands upon, we learned that there was no one in the dún save the servants and a handful of pikes only. Lord Rickard and Lady Amy had gone to Galway two days before, to a feasting of the Governor's, and were returning to Dunkellin this very night. Rickard—so Ruari assured us—had taken a guard of twenty trained men, to accompany them on the road—his Sassenach bodachs in steel and buff—and all mounted.

Donal considered that. "It is not the worst of news," he said at last. "It shows that in Rickard's mind was a march home in the night and the lady with him."

During a meal off a calf which Teig and Ruari had killed and cooked for us, Donal was deep in thought, and in no pleasant thought either, to judge by his drawn-down brows. And indeed I too was thinking seriously. This lady of his in the midst of twenty soldiers, was the kernel of a nut not easy to crack. And crack it we must—or try to. More to myself than to him I spoke aside. "Twenty troopers! Heavy metal for our light horses!"

"This is not worrying me at all," Donal said. "You saw me pick these lads here and I picked them well."

"But an ambush out here——"

"I know. I do not like it. But risk is in it any way you look, and the risk we must take. If you are done eating—and time for you—we will look over the ground."

Father Senan and Teig Ironhand went with us. Teig led seawards for half a mile where the Esker took a curve north and again west. Here we were out of sight of the dún, and went down to the outer edge of the trees, crossed over the bight, and came to the other angle of the ridge. And there was the Galway road. It came in a straight line side by side with the Esker and, at an angle, held straight out over the level until it curved out of sight round a plantation a quarter of a mile across the grass.

Donal looked up at the Esker, he looked along the Galway road, he looked over the sweep of pasture, and made up his mind, his jaws grinding. " Ambush it is," he said in his teeth, " and this is the spot. If Rickard the Sassenach looks for danger he will hardly look for it so near his own dún. Post our men up there in the fringe of the trees—that side of the point—and no one coming on the road can see them without turning to look."

The day wore on, and at last it was dark there on the edge of the trees, and my nerves began to string themselves tightly. The waiting was beginning to tell on me. Eastwards the moon had risen above the Esker, but our angle of the ridge was still in deep shadow except where a thinning of the trees showed a silver gleam among the trunks. The road below us was dark too, for the shadow of the trees still lay far out on the grass. The spread of parkland was a wavering grey shimmer, and the tree clumps lifted out of it like black islands. So bright was the moon that I could see the silver sheen of the sea and make out the black bulk of the cliffs of Clare beyond it. A most quiet and radiant scene under the summer sky ! But here under the fringe of the trees were men strung for the ambush.

Time passed slowly, but—someone was coming down the road, beyond a doubt. There was no mistaking the sound, and in a short while it was certain that many came. There was the confused thud of hooves and now and then the cadence of a voice lifted carelessly. I straightened in the saddle, flexed my knees, and slowly drew my Ferrara. I kept my eyes at the end of the road and steadied my grip on hilt.

And there was a horse's head, and there another. Two riders came abreast—a lady on the inside swaying easily to the walk-amble of her horse, and beyond her a tall man black-bearded. They went by and did not glance our way. My eyes did not follow them. For the head of their escort was coming round the curve, two and two riding abreast, twenty English soldiers all told, slouched wearily in the saddle —riding carelessly at last. Their steel corselets took the gleam of the moon. Here and there a voice murmured, and one man whistled softly. They were so near home, danger behind, supper in front. Poor fighting men !

I eased back in the saddle, lifted my sword slowly, and waited. And then—for I had been chosen leader—brought blade down with a cut that sang—the agreed signal—struck Benmee with knee and heel, felt her jerk and spring, and there was I hurtling down at the head of the column. Thunder of hooves behind me, a startled clatter of hooves on the road, sudden shouts that rose into a shriek, and then Donal's voice like a clarion : " Amy ! Amy ! To me, Amy ! " And then the slogan of the clan like a wolf's howl—" O'Cahan ! O'Cahan ! " And then—all was over !

It was quick as that—quicker than that. Our first onfall had broken Dunkellin's guard beyond all rallying, swept them clean off the road, and they had all taken to flight in their panic ; men on foot running across the grass, scattered horsemen galloping furiously for the dún ! It was all over.

Before I had time to think of Donal I heard the rallying blare of the curved bronze horn that had come down the clan for twenty generations. I kicked Benmee and galloped.

I came on him on the road near the first plantation, sitting finely upright on his horse, broadsword in hand. And by his side sat his lady, tall and slim in her saddle. On the road before them stood a lean man with a black beard, who still gripped the hilt of a broken sword, and by his side stood Father Senan.

Men galloped to us from all parts, and I brought my

mind to my duty. My voice had a deeper note as I marshalled my lads and swung them across the road.

We had won our lady and had Dunkellin himself in our net. And though two or three men had wounds, not a single man was missing.

I swung Benmee round and brought sword to salute. " All present, O'Cahan ! "

Donal saluted back. " It is well. This is my lady."

Again I saluted, and the axe-blades swished to salute behind me. There was a disciplined soldierly silence.

The black-bearded Rickard stood up straight and tall enough, but his head was restless on his shoulders. He lifted his right hand and looked at his broken sword, and then threw the useless weapon furiously on the ground.

Donal spoke a quiet order. " Open ranks, there ! " And then calmly to his enemy. " That is your road, Dunkellin. You are free to go."

Rickard the Sassenach threw a furious gesture towards the lady. " Come, daughter ! " he ordered fiercely.

For answer she put her hand on Donal's arm, and though her voice trembled it was clear and strong. " This is my place now, father."

Still a moment he hesitated, struggling between ire and dignity. Then he swung round suddenly, sent Father Senan staggering, and strode away between the open ranks. There was that in his stride that told us that he would start running as soon as he was out of sight. I heard the lady's voice lifted tremulously. " Let us go from here, Donal. He will loose all Connacht against us."

Donal laughed confidently and comfortingly. " Let him, queen ! We know the safe road, and in a week you will rule us in Dungiven.—Twos-about, David, and let us go."

CHAPTER XIII

THE WEDDING IN THE GLADE

FULL dawn found us deep in the woods north of the Athenry road, and there we made our first halt where a tinkle of water ran under mosses near the ruins of an old Christian, or it might be pagan, shrine. We had camped at this place on the outward ride two nights before and had hidden, in a hole under the brambles, a couple of skins of wine, a bundle of barley scones, and the cooked hind-quarters of a fallow-deer. Besides this provender we had the remnants of Ruari's calf, which reminds me to say that the herd had been released before we left Esker, and had made straight for the Clare fastnesses as the only safe place for him.

Before we set teeth in food Father Senan did his great duty. He washed his hands and his face in the running water, extracted from his satchel a rumpled surplice, a broad purple ribbon, and a thin book with a ragged leather cover, and called his congregation together. And there in that little glade he wedded Donal and his lady. I stood up behind Donal's shoulder, and Teig Ironhand her foster-father stood at Lady Amy's.

When we had eaten a good meal Donal called us all together. " Now, my clan and my children," he said, making a play of words in the Gaelic, " here is where the roads divide, to meet at Samhaoir or at Roe, and God guide us every one. Ye know the rule of old : scatter wide and avoid fight. A dead enemy ties a string to your feet. As we know, the wood-kerns will already be on the trail, and riders gone the open road to warn Cong and Tuam and Athenry. Let not more than two men keep together, for the meshes of the net are close ; but ye have broken many a mesh before now and will again, God aiding. Go then, and remember, my heroes, that ye are hurrying to a wedding-feast at Dungiven, and that the feast will last a day for every day ye have ridden with me on this great venture. God with us ! "

Each man in turn came leading his spent horse, saluted his chief, bent knee to his lady, and was gone. Teig Ironhand came last, and the lady, with an impulsive gesture that I liked, clapped her soft hands each side of his great shaggy head and kissed him on the brow. " Teig, my only father now," she whispered, and for a moment like a child he laid that great head down on her shoulder. Oh, but this was a kind and lovely woman !

Soon, then, were old Father Senan and I setting out together for Dungiven, and we began by turning our faces from it. The good friar led away westwards without any northing, though Dungiven was north and by east, and I made no protest.

" When do we turn north ? " I only put to him.

" As soon as that way is safe. The first drive of pursuit will go that way, and I am seeking to get outside the brunt of it. Since the days of Shane and the coming of the new Church I have once or twice—ay ! four or five times—been hunted—like a wolf—and I ever found it a good rule to follow behind the hounds nosing for me. To-night—and to-morrow—we will keep striking west and by north for the shores of Corrib, slip our way between Cong and Tuam, and make for O'Connor Roe country where my tonsure might save your flaming head."

I ran my fingers through the upthrow of my red hair.

" No ! " said he ; " it is but a warm brown."

And I grinned at the lie.

All night we slowly worked our way north and by west. Our tough little horses had been freshened by the long rest, and we ourselves after a fine sleep and a sound meal were again restrung for the adventures of the road.

An hour after midnight the moon clouded over and the rain came sighing over the woods. That rain held steadily for three hours, and slowed our pace. The rain itself we did not mind. We but wrapped our long cloaks round us, pulled the hoods over head, and the oil-impregnated wool with its skin lining kept us dry and warm. Sometime near dawn we rested against a tree and ate the last of our provisions. I shared a bannock with Benmee and she nibbled it daintily out of my fingers.

At full daylight we examined the country before us from the head of a slope. It lay below us flat and heavily wooded mile after mile, until at last and far away it lifted into a low ridge, bare of trees.

" Corrib Loch is at the other side of that drum," Father Senan told me. " There will be a township or two down there in the woods—which are not as thick as they look—and we must find an Irishman and a Christian sometime to-day or starve. Shall we strike out for a piece ? "

I agreed, and we went down into the plain. But before going the priest wrought a remarkable change in himself. Up to now no one would have discerned in him the churchman—his tonsure hidden under a leather morion with a steel rim ; a war-cloak over his knee-long saffron tunic that was belted with leather instead of the cord of his Order ; and his sparth-axe* never to be mistaken for a crook. But now he hung his morion on the saddle-string and draped cloak over it, and there was the Celtic tonsure from ear to ear, filmed with a ten-days' growth of iron-grey but plain enough. Somehow that tonsure gave his bearded face a certain mildness not noticeable under the morion. He was not done yet. He unbelted his tunic, pulled it over his head, turned it inside out, and there was the habit of his Order, short indeed but of the proper black, with cowl flat on shoulders and cord sewn round waist. Now truly he was a friar and could never have been anything else. He reached me his sparth-axe.

" Sling it this side of your hip," he requested, " and if I have to snatch it—well and good."

* Irish *spairt*, heavy.

" If we meet Bingham's riders now, you will burn," I warned him.

" And you hang. Where the difference ? Let us on."

It was well on in the morning before we came on signs of a township. First we struck a pannier-track leading our way, and this we followed with due precaution, the friar moving ahead at each of its many twists and examining the track beyond before he signalled me to follow. For the better part of an hour we went thus, and then at one wide curve he checked and gestured me aside urgently.

Not far behind him was a low-growing hazel in full verdure, and I swerved Benmee into the shelter of this and peered through the branches at Father Senan's broad back. Beyond him I could see a few yards of the path before it curved out of sight, and on this presently appeared a barefoot Irish villager, a middle-aged man with a dark lean face and a wild-cat-skin cap on his cropped head. He halted before the friar, took off his cap, and bent knee in a short quick bow to the Church's blessing. This portended well and I listened with open ears.

" God and Mary's blessing with you, my son," said the priest in a mild fervour.

" God and Mary with you—and Saint Patrick," came the response.

" Where does this road lead to, my child ? "

" To my township of Bellaghy, reverend Father, a mile back from here in O'Flaherty country."

" Is there a priest with you in that place ? "

" My grief ! no, Father. A true priest has not come our way these months."

" Alas ! for our religion—— "

" Are you looking our way, Father ? " he asked eagerly. " You will be a thousand times welcome."

" Is a Queen's priest with you ? "

" Mary mother ! we are all Catholic, thank God. We are poor, Father, but you will be safe there. No *Sasanach dearg* troubles us these days."

" Then I will come. But there is one with me—a young
brother straight from France—not yet a holy man of Mother
Church, but on the road."

" He will be welcome too, Father."

So I came out from my screen of hazels and saw the surprise
in the villager's eyes. What with my bulk below war-cloak,
my equipment, my feathered bonnet, my days-old scrub on
chin and cheek, I must have looked anything but a man
leaning to holiness. Afterwards the priest denied as much as
a single small lie. His brother was I, as were all men ; my
celibate ways showed a churchly leaning ; and out of France
had I come, if not straight, not unseldom in a hurry.

The villager, Murrigan O'Flaherty Dhu by name, led
us back to his township, and he was a proud man of his
mind. We were indeed very welcome amongst these simple
and primitive clansmen, and it was heartwarming to see
their love and loyalty towards the wandering friar and,
in some reflected degree, towards his brother in disguise.
They regaled us of their best, procured from somewhere a
flagon of Spanish wine in addition to their own heady brew,
piled fresh beds of bracken for us, and permitted no one in
our vicinity while we rested.

And indeed Father Senan did not rest for long. He was
a new man in his priestly calling. Weary and worn as he must
have been, an old man who had borne the strain, he rose to
do his duties finely and tirelessly in that hamlet of lowly
men. In that place that had been without a minister for so
long there was much for him to do : children to be baptised,
couples to wed, the Last Sacrament to be administered to
two or three who were sick, a new house to be blessed, and
the shriving of many who believed themselves to be sinners.
Poor sinners ! There was not amongst them one sinner as
I knew sinners.

CHAPTER XIV

IN DESPERATE STRAITS

A FINE fresh morning it was after a night of rain. The sun was above the trees ; the sky, far and pale and fragile, was without a cloud ; and high up in it a lark soared and sang. Here and there a thin smoke of vapour rose off the wet grass, eddied, quivered, and was gone. And a thrush, after his breakfast, sang six notes of a song.

Above the thrush's singing I heard the sound of running water, and, going that way, came to a dell winding back into the woods with a strong stream purling down it. I followed it up till I reached a small cascade that made a nice pool below, and there I did my toilet. The water was heavy after the rain, but not muddy, and I stripped and plunged into the brisk coolness of it. Thereafter I shaved by touch as I was accustomed to, put on a fresh thin linen under-tunic that I carried in my satchel, washed the used one under the runnel and hung it to dry on a hawthorn. I felt a new man now—skin aglow under fresh linen, chin pleasantly smooth, energy a-leaping in me—and a stomach clamouring for breakfast.

After a fine meal we decided that we would leave the township early in the evening, make for Corrib side, and never cry halt till we were past the danger spot of Cong. But that choice was not long left to us.

There came a stir and flurry outside our door, and in hurried Murrigan Dhu with one of the outposts. These outposts had been set to watch the inlets to the villages. This one had been stationed on the southern track and had a disturbing tale to tell.

He had met one Eoin, son of Gannon, from the township of Clounacaora six miles south, and had learned that a troop of English horse had billeted in that township the previous night. Eoin had been out with the MacWilliams against the English before the truce, and in the night he had stolen away with his neck. The Sassenach were drawing a net through the woods, he said, for the stragglers of a terrible northern raid, while a body of light horse and kern had made a dash to block the Curlew passes. Two hundred of the O'Cahans from north of Tyrone, so the story went, had come like a flame on Dunkellin, put the garrison to the sword, cut out Rickard the Sassenach's tongue, burned down the dun, and were off to the north with the Baron's daughter, twenty maids, and six crocks of gold. Our poor little raid, that had looked so fine and bold, had grown prodigiously in the telling, and I began to think small of myself. We had put a score of English soldiers to flight, stolen one calf, and carried away one willing maiden—nothing to boast about any more.

We did not tarry long in Bellaghy after that news. We made our churchly calling an excuse for haste ; and the clansmen, whether they suspected us or not, did all they could to set us on our way. In less than a quarter-hour we were mounted, the priest had given his final blessing, and we were a-gallop out of the hamlet north and by west.

Father Senan had re-turned his tunic, and his bearded face was stern under its morion. " You see," he explained with grim humour, " if it comes to the bit I would rather hang than burn."

And indeed we got overclose to a hanging that day.

We had ridden an hour at a speed to conserve our horses, but we were not as watchful of the road in front as we should have been. We looked for danger from the rear, and kept eyes backwards wherever the ground gave us prospect. Thus it was we came ambling down a brae, round a clump of briar, and out on a wide wagon-road. And there, not two hundred paces on our right, was half a troop of English horse advancing towards us at a foot pace.

Things happened quickly after that. We did not wait to count the enemy. The shout they gave seemed to act as a spur to our mounts, and we were across the road and into the trees at top speed before they had set hooves a-clattering. We rode full gallop up a long glade, swerved with it to the left, and there, full in our path, was a big man on a big horse, a giant fellow in buff with a peaked casque above his eyes.

" We're for it ! " Andrea Ferrara grated and sang out of scabbard. I was riding half a length behind and holding Benmee in. Now I gave her knee and she was abreast. " I will take him," I shouted to the priest. " You keep on."

The trooper faced us solidly in the middle of the glade, and already his sword was out. I was close to him before I saw who it was. Tom Pybus ! the man I had drawn sword on twice already. " At last ! " was the thought in my head. " One of us will kill the other this time."

But neither of us did. I suppose the big fellow knew that he was slow with his weapon and that I overmatched him, or it might be that he had no mind to press me. Instead of using his weight to charge me down he reined his horse stiffly and, as I came at him, his blow was hesitating and loose-handed. I parried so fiercely that the hilt was jarred out of his grip, and there he was at my mercy. He swayed his head and shoulders away from me, and I had only to run him through the body. I could not. Instead I thrust foot under his and shot him clean out of the saddle. And he had not thudded on the ground before I had bundled by and was up with the priest, who had checked his horse and armed himself with sparth.

" *Mhuire !* " he cried ; " you killed him."

" You could not kill that man."

I glanced over shoulder, and there once more was Tom Pybus trundling after his horse. I had to laugh.

" He fell like a sack of stones," called the priest. " Was it the hilt ? "

I shook head. " Press on ! Luck comes with him always."

But our luck did not overtake us yet. We laboured slant-wise to the head of a long rise ; below us was a shallow valley, and beyond it a stiff brae jutted with black and coloured limestones. The bottom of the valley was a chain of thick clumps of blackthorn and bramble with a gleam of running water showing between. We raced down the slope, the air singing in our ears, broke between two clumps and came to a racking halt on the brink of a brawling torrent, brown and swollen by the rain.

That torrent was not more than a dozen long paces wide, but it doomed us more surely than a great river. For the depth and rush of it between tilted slabs of stone made it wholly impassable—mounted or on foot.

To our right it slanted away from our pursuers who were still over the ridge, and in a last effort we forced our horses that way through the undergrowth. In less than a minute we came to where it again curved back, and mid-way in the curve a great shelf of limestone shouldered out of the rush of water. It was some four yards out from the high bank on our side. Father Senan in after days computed it six or maybe seven spades, and used to boast that while I jumped the whole way he jumped most of it. Between us and that slab the water ran deep and strong, but beyond to the shelving bank it appeared fordable. I looked at the torrent and it was for-bidding. I looked at the stone and I liked it better. It offered a chance of escape and we had no time to look for a safer one.

I hurled myself off Benmee and slapped her on the withers. " Good-bye, lassie ! You carried me well." There was little time for farewell.

Father Senan was at my side. " I can never do it, David," he cried.

" Do it we must," I shouted above the rush of the waters. " Stand back ! "

The undergrowth gave me two short paces. I twisted

cloak under arm, gripped my sword-scabbard high, took the quick kick-and-jerk of the hop-step-and-leap—and leaped. The stone jarred me to the neck, my feet slipped into the water, but already my hands were secure on a jut of rock and I pulled myself to security. Father Senan was on the brink, looking down on me and shaking his head.

"Throw me your axe," I shouted to him, and that he did. I grasped the jut of rock with one hand, grasped the socket of the axe with the other, and reached the four-foot handle as far as I was able. "Jump!" I dared him furiously. "Jump—and drown—or hang! Jump!"

Later, he said it was the fury in my eyes that compelled him. He pressed the morion down on his head, gathered his cloak, and threw himself forward. He clutched hands at the axe-haft and soused under. The shock of his weight all but wrenched my fingers from axe and rock, but luckily the rush of water and my pull carried him round to the back-swirl behind the shelf, and there I held and hauled him, got a hold of his collar, and dragged him face-down to precarious safety.

He spluttered through bearded lips, winked the water out of his eyes, and stared at me speechlessly. I gave him no time to get wind or tongue back, but caught him round the waist, cloak and all, and plunged feet first into the rush beyond the rock. We found bottom knee-deep; the water ridged up our thighs, but our solid weight withstood the pressure, and we made the other bank in one desperate splashing rush. And it was then we heard the shouting behind us; and there came a scurry of horsemen down the slope.

"David," cried my stout old warrior, "with axe and sword we could hold this against them."

"Not against arquebus. Come on!"

We faced the shelving bank and the rock-jutted brae above and started the slow climb. What risk or safety was beyond we did not know—nor care very much then. Our pace was tardy now. The old priest who, on horseback, had stood the strain with the best, was short of wind and limb and was soon spent amongst those slippery bosses of sun-hot stone. He lagged and I waited for him.

" Oh, Davy ! Davy ! " he panted. " I am old and done. Be not minding me. You are young—you make on——."

In reply I caught him at the belt and pulled him in front of me. Then indeed I should have thanked God for strength of body and lung. But I had no time, and I needed all that was in me for the work in hand. In a little while the old man could do no more than keep feet under him, and I pushed him upwards like an unwieldly sack.

Three-quarter-way up I was forced to halt. Face-down over a rock, I struggled to get my breath, and never before in my life did I experience that terrible whooping indraw that fails to fill the lungs. I thought my heart would burst.

The priest lay against me, speechless, and gently patted my shoulder. " Look ! " he whispered at last.

CHAPTER XV

KILLER COSBY AGAIN !

DOWN below us many horsemen were forcing a way along the torrent-side, looking for a crossing-place, but none had yet ventured our road. One man directly below us had dismounted and was busy over the primings of an arquebus. I filled my lungs once again and resettled my grip. The old man groaned with the effort and we resumed the climb— slowly and slowly. We were near the head of the brae when the tensely-waited-for bellow roared behind us and the lead spattered the rock at our side. We were over the top before another shot could be fired.

There we halted, drawing in the air open-mouthed, the blood hissing in my ears, my head dizzy, sweat salt on my lips ; and, once open, our mouths stayed open and our eyes stared in front of us. For there before us was the wide reach of Loch Corrib, the water we had been trending towards so eagerly for two days, and now it hemmed us in and betrayed us. We stood at one horn of a deep bay, and on our right hand where we had hoped to hide in the woods was a mile-wide stretch of deep water. We could not hope to get round the detour of that inlet before our pursuers found a road to us.

Corrib is a great expanse of inland sea, a good thirty miles in length and, at this point, some three miles across. The far shore lifted into a fine wooden ridge, gapped by the gash of an inlet going back into the breast of big hills— great purple masses of hill, peaceful and remote under the high summer sky. Over there was safety ; here death was at our heels and, between, Corrib waters shimmered in the sun.

" David, son," said my old friend stilling his panting breath, " I am old and done and this fate had to overtake me soon or late. But you are young.—Look ! if you hurry now you might get round that bluff and win clear. Never mind me—I can hold them a while."

I looked at him sullenly.

" Up or down they will find a road," he urged, " and why should two of us suffer ? There is no more good in me."

A hot anger came over me. Had the old man no sense ? How could I face Dungiven and the soldierly men who held it, knowing that I had left the old priest to die ?

" I will not part with you this day," I said. " Come. We will work round by the trees close to the water."

So we went down the slope, linked together. And we did not hurry. The old friar could not, and since I was tied to him irrevocably a mood of desperate quietness came to me. No, not quietness ! A strange satisfying humour that gave me a sense of pride in myself. By the goodness of God, if we were going to die we would die side by side, and my name and nation would not be a byword in the mouths of men.

So we came to the trees, went quietly through them, and came round a patch of wild raspberries above the fine gravel of the shore. And there a tall man, leaning to pick a berry, started upright and swore a sudden short oath.

We were startled too. I swung the priest aside and grasped at my hilt. And, grasping it, I had Andrea Ferrara out and on guard. For one glance told me who this man was.

He was Captain Sir William Cosby of Cong, the slayer of Colum O'More. Here now was death close to us—and to him. My mind leaped to the conclusion that he was here with his men and that the end had come for us.

" Draw ! " I said in my throat. " I will kill you this day before I die. Draw, you swine ! "

His hand was at his hip, but only a dagger was there. He was not even in his soldier's dress, but wore a doublet and hose of black and red and, instead of a casque, a flat-topped slashed cap. As I came at him he snatched at his poor weapon, gave back a step, and crouched on guard, but in his glazed eye was the knowledge that death was at his throat. It was so easy to break through that guard. It was too easy. I hesitated.

And as I hesitated a woman screamed at my left hand. And though she screamed she was bold. She came round the raspberry canes like the wind and, unhesitatingly, drove between Cosby and me. My flickering blade was not a hand's-breadth from her shoulder. She looked from one to the other. " What is it ? " Her breath was drawn in sharply. " What is it, Captain Cosby ? "

A young maid she was and bonny too. I could note that, even in the stress of passion. Not very tall, with black hair waving and the good blood not yet ebbed from her cheeks. Frightened she might be, but not dismayed, though Father Senan says that my ferocious mien should have terrified any Christian maid.

" Who is it, Captain Cosby ? " she asked again. " Who is this man ? "

" A rebel outlaw," said Cosby, swallowing his palate.

But I was no longer paying attention to man or maid. They were of no interest any more. For, glancing by her shoulder, my eyes saw something that made my heart jump. Down at the edge of the water was a small fishing-boat— a lovely, shapely, God-sent small boat painted green and white. There it was. I blinked my eyes to make sure of it.

I glanced at the priest. His eyes were on it too. I bellowed at him. " Go on ! She is ours."

Life had come back to my old Trojan. He hesitated not at all. He scurried. He clattered on the gravel, shoved the boat's head off, fell over the bow, scrambled to a thwart, grasped oars, and with a practised flick had her stern on to the shore. " Come on, my hero ! " he roared, a fine vigour in his voice. " Ours she is."

Cosby growled like a hound and would have been at the old man, but in two long strides I half-circled the maid and was between him and the boat. My sword was at his throat. " Move, you dog, and die," I threatened, tongue and blade urgent. " Move. Oh, move ! "

The flaxen moustache that bushed up over his cheeks twitched and his teeth showed. But he did not move. Step by step I went backwards to the gravel. I was taking no risks now.

And again this young woman flew lightly between us, and now, instead of fright, there was the flare of battle in her eye. " You hulking red savage," she cried, " that boat is mine ! "

I retreated steadily and she faced close to me.

" Dare you steal it ? "

I was on the gravel now.

" You will hang—— "

" Without it," I finished for her.

She must have seen that I was past moving, and for the

first time she showed dismay. She threw her hands out in an impulsive gesture and her eyes widened.

" But I must be home."

" Walk," said I.

" To the other shore ? "

A long walk surely.

" You brute ! " Anger and dismay in her tone. " I must be home. My mother—— " She wrung her hands and half-turned from me.

My heels splashed in the water and I paused before I swung for the boat. I paused because, before she turned away, I saw real fear in that maid's eye, and something that was almost a prayer to Heaven—or to me. " Mother Mary ! " I caught that desperate whisper.

And then and there I acted on impulse. Maybe it was not impulse after all, but a sudden knowledge that it was not right to leave the maid alone in this wilderness. I strode at her, caught her round the waist with my left arm, lifted her high, pounded into the water, and dropped her without ceremony into the bow of the boat behind the priest.

" Home to your mother, vixen," I cried, " and keep better company." I dragged at the gunwale and vaulted clean over the oar into the stern. That maid had not once screamed or struggled in my arm.

It was then that Cosby made a final essay. He rushed forward into the water, growling, dagger lifted, teeth bare, and forthwith I did my very utmost to get him. I put arm and shoulder behind that long lunge. He braked himself desperately, head thrown back, and the drag of the water on his feet helped. My point just reached him below the breastbone, and steel jarred on steel. It was true then that he wore mail. The shock knocked him flat on his back with a great splash.

" Ah ! He is spitted," cried the priest.

" No ! but he will be," I shouted, and then and there would have leaped back and pinned his throat to the gravel.

But at that the oarsman tugged full strength, the boat shot out into the loch, and I fell breast down on the sternboard, my long blade trailing in the water.

The flurry and the fury were not yet finished. As I scrambled to my knees a great shout burst from the hill and men on foot came pouring down to the loch-side. Three were well ahead : two troopers armed with arquebus and a tall officer carrying a naked sword. The foremost soldier plunged through the water till it reached his hips, levelled his piece and pulled trigger. He had aimed low, for the bullet cut the water one side of the stern and went singing off into the air.

" Oh ! Coward ! Coward ! " cried Father Senan. "And a lady with us ! "

The second trooper pulled up on shore, looked at his priming, and brought his weapon to the level. I turned to the maid in the bow. " Down ! " I ordered her, and she crouched her dark head to the gunwale. Some instinct brought me to my feet to draw the bullet high. But the bellow of the explosion never came. For the tall officer came bounding behind the man, struck him a mighty blow under the ear, and laid him flat on the gravel. I knew that tall officer. He was Sir Francis Vaughan.

A fine warmth surged in me. "A Vaughan ! A Vaughan ! " I cheered him, cap doffed. " My fine man of the English ! "

He lifted his hand and waved to me.

CHAPTER XVI

EITHNE O'FLAHERTY

BACK there on land there had been hot stress in plenty, and now we had snatched ourselves clean out of it and away from it. We were a distance from the shore, and suddenly as it seemed a great quietness had come about us. There was only the click and feather of the oars and a soft gurgle at the

bows, and all about us was the wide reach of Corrib rippling
in the soft breeze and shimmering under the sun. I sat in the
stern and looked at the priest pulling.

He was a good oarsman but his wet clothes hindered him.
Moreover, his cheeks above beard were strangely pale and
his breath blew through his lips. So I slipped off my cloak,
and placing my hands over his, stopped the sway of his body.
We changed places.

As I sidled by him in that swaying little craft I glanced
at the maid, who was now sitting up in the bow. She had
uttered no word yet and now she did not even glance at me.
Her eyes were across the water to the group on the shore,
and a frown of some perplexity was on her brow.

I was not so deft with my oars as Father Senan, but I
had strength and again my wind ; and I lifted the boat
through the water at a fine surge direct for the Connemara
shore. The sooner we got there the better, though our pursuers
had a twenty-mile circuit to reach us.

The old man made himself comfortable in the stern,
eased his heart with two or three deep breaths, and bethought
himself of his calling. He looked up at the sun-full sky.
" Glory to God and His Blessed Mother, and all the Saints,"
he gave thanks, " that saved our lives this day ! "

" And a saint or two with us for a small while yet," I
added prudently.

He smiled at me, his eyes wet. " And a small meed of
thanks to one David Gordon too." He pulled off his close-
fitting morion and rubbed his hand over his steaming
tonsure.

And at last the maid behind me spoke. " Why ! " she cried
in some surprise, " you are a priest after all."

" And a poor sinner as well," he said. And added, " You
need have no fear, my daughter."

" I am not afraid," she denied. " I never was afraid."
She said it proudly.

" You will forgive us, my daughter," said my wise old man.

" We had to do it. We were flying for our lives from the English soldiery—— "

" Why ? Because you are a priest ? "

" There was another reason too—and if anything it was a better reason."

" But how should I know ? " she made complaint. " This ruffler brandishing a sword before a man defenceless—if he had said but a word ! "

I made the boat leap. Here was feminine malice.

But my old friend had a salty tongue too.

" He is a very hasty young man, this young man, surely," he said, mildly sardonic. " A great pity the four of us did not sit down to it—and the day so fine ! "

" But there was no call for swashbuckling," she gave back spiritedly.   And though you may be a priest, a wolf sometimes puts on sheep's clothing—with his brother the red wolf."

My sorrow ! but she was quick as an adder that day.

" Our acts belie us, my daughter," said the priest quietly, " and we hope to prove that to you. If you tell us where you live we will row you as near as we may with safety— and be thanking you a thousand times."

After a pause she told him. " That gap opening between Inish—between these two islands. In there."

I turned to look where she pointed and I saw the mouth of an inlet open between rocky bluffs. It was still a long mile away and some distance to my left, and I set the boat's head for it.

" Cashlean-na-Kirka, the dún of the great Captain Dame Bevinda O'Flaherty, is somewhere in there ? " half-queried the priest.

" She is my mother," said the maid. " I am her daughter Eithne."

" At your service, my lady," he gave back a trifle blankly.

All Gaeldom had heard of Queen's Captain Dame Bevinda O'Flaherty of Cashlean-na-Kirka. A widowed great lady with one daughter and a mind of her own. Because of some private quarrel with the MacWilliams and the O'Kellys she had armed her stronghold with a culverin or two, garrisoned it with a standard of ferocious O'Flahertys, and held it against all comers. And then she made petition to Elizabeth the English Queen for permission to do these things she had already done. "Bevinda!" said that Queen, reading out the strange name and swearing a customary oath: "'Sdeath! but these wild Irishmen have outlandish names. Bevinda! Still the man is well disposed, and in our grace we will make him a Captain." So the Dame got her Captain's commission and was more than equal to it. And though men laughed there was no ridicule in their mirth, for Captain Bevinda was as good as any man of her clan, and the men of her clan knew themselves to be a shade better than the best.

And here now was her dark-haired daughter whose boat we had pirated, whose self we had carried off, who was powerful enough to double and more than double the mounting dangers of the road—and we rowing directly into the jaws of the tigress. I slowed down my rate of rowing and was not at all happy in my mind. For, however I looked at it, I could not see this insulted daughter do anything kindly towards one man she had lately called a hulking red savage and another she had but now hinted to be a wolf in sheep's clothing.

And then a fine memory struck me. Had I not heard Donal Ballagh, that last night at Dungiven, speak of a visit to Cashlean-na-Kirka, where he met his lady? I had—and now I chose my words carefully.

"This lady," said I, looking at Father Senan intently, "is a friend of her who was Amy Burke."

He stared at me in complete amazement, his face vacant of all but surprise. Before the import of my words could reach him the maid behind me spoke quickly, anxiously.

"Amy Burke—my friend—who was?"

Then he got it. His eyes beamed on me. " My darling fellow ! " he cried. " My sound man ! The rope is not made would hang us, nor the tree planted to make a faggot for our burning." He smiled at the maid over my shoulder. " Your friend is well, my lady," he told her. " But she is no longer Amy Burke."

At once she knew what he meant. " Oh ! " she cried high and happily, and I heard her hands clap together. " Has she got her gallant young O'Cahan ? "

" She has surely—her own Donal Ballagh." He looked at me gratefully. " This my friend is David Gordon, his own cousin ; and in religion my name is Senan. I married the young pair yesterday in the woods north of Athenry, and they are off north for Dungiven. It is a great tale."

" How splendid ! " Her voice was warm and glad. I drew a deep breath of relief. I could feel the new mood that came about us. She was so eager that she forgot for the time the hulking red savage. " Why," she cried, " I was with Amy that morning our plans failed us—and I was with her two nights ago at Bingham's feast. Tell me, father."

He cleared his throat like the story-teller he was, and a wicked humour made me laugh at him. I glanced at the eager maid over my shoulder and she caught my red eyes.

" A brief tale," said I, " and easily told. Two hundred men of the O'Cahans, as well as a red savage and an old done friar, raided down from Dungiven, put the Dunkellin garrison to the sword, cut out Rickard the Sassenach's tongue, burned his dún, and made off north with his daughter, twenty maids, and six crocks of gold. That is all."

" Oh ! " breathed the lady weakly.

The priest laughed. " Never mind what he says, Lady Eithne. He is only retelling some of the wild rumours that are already gone abroad. This is the true tale."

And there and then, as I drew steadily on the oars, he told the tale and he told it well. He began it at Dungiven

with the message that came for Donal and he finished it
at Corrib shore ; and like all good story-tellers he added
an inch here and there to stress the risk and the daring. But
foolishly and for no reason at all he would dwell on what he
called my leadership in the ambush—until I could stand it
no longer.

" Bah ! " said I. " What saw you—and you hiding in
your bush ? "

But the lady was eager to hear, and hear it all. She did
—and some besides. But at the very end she surprised the
story-teller. " Oh ! " she cried, pain in her voice. " The
pity that you should spoil it all for me at the end ! " She
brought her palms together. " Why the threatening sword
and the terrible words ? If I—if you told me——".

" My dear daughter," placated the priest hastily, " before
we saw you we saw this Captain Cosby ; and we thought
we were only deeper in the net with his soldiers all round us.
And forget not, Lady Eithne, that though sword was drawn
no blood was spilt, thanks to God."

" Who was this man—this Colum O'More that was
killed ? " she asked the priest.

" Of Offaly—a noble friend to the North."

" In fair fight ? "

He looked at me troubledly.

" He was my friend."

" But a soldier has to fight," she cried, almost plaintively,
" and sometimes to slay. Captain Cosby is a soldier—hard,
but a great fighter for his Queen—and my—my mother's
friend. Why this ugliness of killing ? "

If Cosby was her friend, or her mother's friend, I could
say nothing. My dour silence was too much for her. As
I glanced over my shoulder to get a line on the approaching
inlet I saw that her head was down in thought. And when
next I glanced round she was sitting aside looking at the
shore now close ahead. The arm of the loch opened between
its guarding islands and I straightened bow for it.

" No," she said quietly. " Your left oar. We take the
shore channel."

I did as she bid and came inside the rocky tip of an island.
The channel was not more than arrow-flight wide and
shoal water.

" Close inshore," she directed me. " We can be seen
here."

I looked back up a deep inlet, and a mile away on the
other side of the shore was a tall, strong grey tower standing
above the water on a bare promontory.   Behind it rose a
wooded hill and above that a brown ridge gashed by a
corrie.*

I pulled strongly for the land, here heavily wooded to the
water's edge, and skirted along on the fringe of the trees.
The strong tower was now hidden behind a nose of land,
and on our rounding that it still remained hidden by another
farther on. Between the two points a bonny inlet was thrust
in among the hills.

" In here," said the lady shortly.

The thought came to me that in here we were on the
wrong side of the main inlet to make good our escape. But
I said nothing, and did as I was bid. At the head of the
water a strong stream came down brawling from the hills—
and a prime trout-stream by the look of it. The lady's hand
directed me, and we grated to shore just outside the outward drive of the current. At once I jerked in the oars,
stepped over the side into a few inches of water, and lifted
the bow to the gravelly edge of the beach. I stood within
hand-reach of the maid, but she looked past me at Father
Senan and spoke quietly to him : " Ye will be safer for the
present this side of the loch—if ye trust me."

" With our lives—and in your hands they are, my lady."

" The soldiers will be looking for you on the other side.
Listen, then.   You see this stream—the Glosha.   There
is your road. Follow it up into the hills—four miles it might

* A hollow recess on a mountain-side.

be and not a hard road. Half-way up you will strike the pannier-track from Cashlean—at Glounamaol—and following that you will come to the deer-warden's bothy in the Glen of the Echo. Tell old Garrodh that I sent you. He lives alone with his hounds—and you will be safe with him. No one goes that road while the stags are still in velvet.* And note this : he has never forgiven my mother for being known as a loyalist. Food he will have—it might be venison, for some-times, he says, a hart breaks a leg slipping on the Linen Apron†—which is a lie, I think. In the morning at the latest more will be sent—and the way may be open for you. Now you must hurry—and I must hurry too."

"Oh, kind one of the heart ! " The old man's voice was vibrant. "Lucky the day we met you ! "

He scrambled stiffly over the thwart, and I gave him shoulder and arm to the gravel. There he turned and took the lady's hand : "God and Mary with you, O Queen of Connacht ! " She reached hands for the oars. The priest stamped across the gravel to the grassy shore, and I grated the boat out into the water. There she deftly swung the little craft stern round and looked at me evenly for the first time. Then I drove myself to do the right thing.

I strode into the water knee-deep and took off my feathered bonnet. I laid a holding hand on the stern. "My lady," said I, "I ask your forgiveness. I am sorry that I hurt you."

"You did me no hurt, sir." She smiled suddenly. "As for forgiveness, Master Gordon," she said, "I forgave you long ago." Then she leant forward and spoke in a low voice that the priest might not hear. "Your old friend, I think, will not be fit for travel for a day or two. A priest, he will be safe with us, but there is no need for you to stay."

I glowered at her from under sullen brows. Would she, too, have me forsake this my old hero ?

"For him there is no danger," she replied to that glower,

---

* Antlers not yet grown.   † The "Linen Apron" was the name given to a foaming waterfall in the district.

" but for you there must be. Yet I know you will not leave him though you die."

The oars ridged the water, the stern slipped from under my hand, and she left me there watching her.

CHAPTER XVII

THE QUEEN OF THE GLEN

WE took near on two hours to reach the deer-warden's bothy in the Glen of the Echo above Glounamaol, and this though the road was no rugged one. The old Father had been pressed too hard, and though he hid his weariness under a gay humour and all his many halts were to admire the bonny trout-pools and fishing-runs so plentiful along the stream, he made no remonstrance when I gave him a hand over the steeper bits.

The bothy was much bigger and more comfortable than the common hunting-bothy. It was built roughly of stone slabs, clinched with clay and thatched with long heather. An open porch faced the pony track, and in there was the hounds' sleeping place.

And, strange enough in a hill-bothy, the two small windows were glazed in green glass. During the hunting season the chieftainess and her guests used it for days at a time, and this accounted for its size and fittings.

The deer-warden was soon appraised of our coming. The approaching path was in view of the bothy for its whole length, and we had not taken a hundred strides on it before the boom of a great dog's barking filled the bowl.

" He is for taking no chances, this old fellow named Garrodh," said Father Senan. " Look at him."

We were near enough to see that he had armed himself with a long-bow taller than himself, and ready strung, and that though he leant on it easily his feet were set in the

4

archer straddle. And when we came nearer we saw the
feathered end of an arrow peeping from under his arm.

An old man he was, but straight and not lean : with
great hunches of shoulders, a sandy beard, and eyes washed
clean of blue, so light were they. His great hand grasping
the bow was like a ham in size and colour.

" God and Mary with you, O son ! " saluted the priest.

" And Saint Patrick with you—Father ! " he responded
in a surprisingly high voice. But he made no move to welcome
us. After all, not every man with a shaven pate might be
trusted, and shaven pate's companion did not look other than
a wolf.

" You will be Garrodh the deer-warden ? "

" Garrodh, son of Garrodh, descendant of Eochy, who
died on the field of Athenry."

" Rest his soul ! " prayed the priest. " And now, Garrodh,
your young mistress, Lady Eithne, when she saved our lives
in her white and green boat, said ' Go to Garrodh the deer-
warden. There you will be safe.' "

Garrodh threw the strung bow over his arm. " Could
you not have said that before, holy man ? " he cried, striding
forward and tendering the hand of welcome. " Here you will
be safe, or nowhere safe. Come away in."

As I entered the front door behind the old hunter I saw
the back door over his shoulder, and as I looked, it closed
the last few inches slowly—just as if someone had pulled it to
carefully behind him.

Garrodh treated us in princely fashion, and by that time
we needed his generosity. There was no venison, but there
was mountain mutton with oaten cakes, butter that had
been cheese-seasoned in a peat-hag, and milk lashed with
usquebaugh. And, eating done, he built up the fire of bog-
pine and peat ; and soon the old priest, busy at his tale, sat
in an armed-chair before the glow, clad only in Garrodh's
woollen cloak while his own clothes were steaming at one
side. Though my horse-boots had been water-filled more than

once that day I did not yet remove them, and I kept sword behind my hip out of sight. The memory of that closing door stayed with me.

In time, with an excusing word I got up and went out the front door. Two hounds were in the porch and one of them came and smelled my long boots. I flicked a finger and he lifted massive head to my palm. " Come, lad," I invited and he followed a few paces, thought better of it and went back to his post.

Quietly I walked round the cow-byre and found that the back door of the bothy led into a deep fold that curved back over the rim of the valley. I went along this fold until it led out into thick heather, and there before me was the true wilderness. A wide, savage, sterile glen sloped up and up into the face of a great hill that was darker than purple, and the whole floor of the glen was a jumble of immense grey boulders. There an army might lie hidden, and if anyone had come out the back door he was safe from all searching.

I stood for a time knee-deep in the tussocks, looking up that savage and lonely valley, and was about to turn away when a movement in the heather caught my eye. No breath of air had stirred, yet over there a little way a tuft swayed aside just as if a hand had moved it to make a peep-hole.

I hesitated not at all. I walked slowly forward, not ever placing hand on hilt. " Up ! " I spoke softly. " There is no fear." And the heather shook and a man scrambled to his feet.

" Cathal O'Dwyer ! " I cried then. " My own friend ! "

" Brother ! " Wistfully welcome was his smile. " You have the hillman's eye."

Cathal O'Dwyer of the Glens it was, the kinsman of Colum O'More whom Cosby had foully slain ; but a Cathal woefully changed. His fine mop of flaxen hair was tousled and lustreless, his face worn thin, his saffron tunic loose on the broad bone of his shoulders. His right arm was bandaged across his breast and the end of a wooden splint showed on the back of his hand.

I strode forward and placed my hand gently on his shoulder.
" A long way from home, Cathal, friend," said I, " but glad
am I to see you."

" Far and far," said he, his voice shaken ; " but where
else would I be ?   Cosby the Killer still lives."

" You are hurt ? "

" His work. He wears a chain shirt next his skin. I had
him at *scian*-point and broke blade on him—not far from
here. I escaped into the woods, but he did this with a French
pistol. This is a known refuge and Garrodh set the bone.
But I think that I was not in my own mind for many days.
I am better now—and better seeing you, David Gordon."

But indeed he was not well. His shoulder was shaking
under my hand. I took his sound arm. " Come ! The man
with me is a priest and leal to the bone."

As we walked down the fold I was perplexed and troubled.
This man, given a fair chance, would slay Cosby—and Cosby
deserved slaying. Yet the Lady Eithne—or her mother—
thought highly of him. How highly ? Ah, well ! It was
none of my business till I found that out.

I slept well, and did not dream of running water or green
seas roaring. Senan and I lodged in the inner-room of the
bothy, while Garrodh and O'Dwyer made beds of heather
and their cloaks in the kitchen. Once or twice in the night I
thought I heard the old priest groan at my side. When I
waked in the daylight I found him lying on his back, but not
sleeping, and there was a twist on his face this fine morning.

" Slugabed ! " and my hand reached for his shoulder.

" No, lad ! " and he winced. " My old enemy is on me,
and I knew it would." And seeing the concern in my face,
he added hastily, " It is nothing—only a stitch that plagues
me whenever I get wet all over or go angling too early of a
spring."

" Where is it ? "

" Here—below the small of the back and across—like a
knife if I move—worse it has been often."

" Ah ha ! " said Garrodh, who had come into the room. " It grips you. Well I know the twist, but in this house is the thing will burn it out of you in three days."

" Burn ! You—— "

" Protect us all ! It is only the first run of the still and warmer than new wool. Wait you and see."

We fed him sparingly out of prudence and then turned him, protesting furiously, on his face while Garrodh rubbed into the affected place a cloudy liquid with a pungent odour. The great fleshy hand moved with a surprising gentleness, and whether it was the soothing or the liquid, our patient was much relieved of his pain.

Safely on his back, he stopped a groan and smiled at me. " That is better. But, son, it will be the best part of a week before I can march."

" There is no hurry on ye, surely," said Garrodh hospitably.

" I know, my friend. But in the heart of Connacht there is always danger for a man of Ulster, and Cosby the Killer I do not trust. Look, Davy ! As a priest I am safe, since Captain Dame Bevinda is loyal to the Church ; but a young lad in a feathered bonnet, with a mile of sword at hip, is in the mouth of danger. You are used to the open, and oh ! the long legs of you ! In four days now you could make O'Donnell's line. That is sense—is it not, Garrodh ? "

" Sound sense enough," admitted Garrodh ; " but he is welcome here."

I shook fist under my old man's nose. " I will stay," said I, " and drown you in the first peat-hole we come to, so that I can tell Dungiven what fate took you."

Ten days we stayed in the Glen of the Echo, and I know now that there was no need on us to stay longer than half that time. Whether it was the salving with raw spirit or his eagerness to be at the fishing, brave Senan was hobbling about on the third day, fishing on the fourth, and fishing every day after that ; and he and Garrodh failed to convince the other as to the superior merit of lure or worm. In my opinion Garrodh was the more adept on his own water, but I did not say so.

Eithne O'Flaherty visited us every day, riding across from Cashlean-na-Kirka on her pony, its panniers laden with delicacies for the sick priest—on one side perhaps a brace of cold fowl and a pasty, and on the other some flagons of Bordeaux wine. Sometime she shared in our feastings and joined us in our fishing excursions to the stream, laughing and talking gaily, and teasing me now and then on my native dourness. She was the queen of this our valley, and we were her loyal subjects. A pleasant and happy maid, and likeable. Bonny she was too.

Old Garrodh, I think, could say his prayers to her— his heart, his light, his brightness of the world. O'Dwyer used to watch her dumbly out of his own subdued and ghostly world ; the good priest wondered how such a one could be born on top of rude earth, and how, being born, could grow in sweetness yet became noble, and being so noble could be so full of charity to hunted men.

And so came the ninth day and the end of this our kingdom.

That day Eithne did not come in the morning. Nor did she come at noon or in the afternoon. But when the sun was already reddening she came riding hurriedly. There was some ebb of colour from her face and her eyes had a dark glow, but gay and gallant were her head and her voice.

" My reign, alas ! is coming to an end," she cried ; " and this my kingdom perishes. A lost glen—a stony valley——water singing to itself alone. Where is my holy man ? "

" Here, my queen," said he, coming out of the door.

" Are you fit for the road, Father ? "

" Any road—or the one to the World's End."

" To-morrow night must it be then." She spoke quickly. " My mother talks of coming to see Garrodh and I think that she has a suspicion. I have been careless, I fear, and she knows that I am in this glen every day. That she would

know, for nothing can be hidden in her own house. Someone followed me yesterday, and what was seen I do not know.
But do not fear. She is frank and noble too, and will do
nothing by stealth. To-morrow—to-night, if she questions
me, there is nothing I can or would hide, but you must be
ready. She takes the raid on Rickard the Sassenach lightly
and says he deserved what befell him—that he is not worthy
of alliance with the O'Cahans. Listen, now. David, you
will meet me to-morrow—an hour after dawn—at the mouth
of the Glosha. I will row the boat across and we will hide it
under the bushes. Then at the first dark of the evening you
will go down ; and Garrodh—are you there, Garrodh ?
You will row them to the north side—to the spring of Tubber-
glass. You know it ? "

"Well I know it, my heart."

"There and nowhere else. Now I shall have to hurry.
I could not get away till my mother was at the milking
bawn, and I fear she will miss me. No, David, you must
not come. I will ride hard all the way. In the morning—
at the Glosha," she repeated, and was gone.

In the half-dark of the summer night Garrodh, rowing
softly, brought us to shore amongst a jumble of rocks where
a spring ran down over green mosses and tinkled murmuringly
as it fell. There was deep water close in and I was able to
land on a flat boulder, while the old friar, sighing to himself,
stumbled against the gunwale and handed me out our well-
stored satchels. Then I helped him ashore, and we buckled
ourselves for the road. Garrodh was leaning at the bow,
holding the rock, and there the priest gave him his final
blessing and I bent down and took his great hand silently.

"Ye will go in safety," he whispered. "In my bones I
feel it—and I know, too, that you will come this way again
and you not hiding."

His words heartened me. I straightened up and turned
away—and then goose-flesh shivered over me. For a hooded
woman was there before us and she had made no sound.

Eithne O'Flaherty ! Well I knew her, though her face was only a pale oval in the half-light.

" Come ! " she whispered to us and leant towards the boat.

" Garrodh, wait for me." She caught the priest's sleeve. " There is no need to hurry now."

She led the way on a path amongst the rocks and we kept close behind. Beyond was a bare patch, and then a copse of hazel with the beginning of a track winding up a brae towards the open. And bridle-tethered to the hazel branches were two horses.

" You know them ? " she whispered.

One was the priest's thick garran. The other was my own bonnie mare Benmee. She knew me before I spoke. As I untied the reins she snorted softly into my face and muzzled me with her small shapely head.

" Lassie—lassie ! " I greeted the mare. " You the darling ! " and rubbed between her ears.

Eithne laughed lowly. " Your gallant enemy Sir Francis Vaughan brought her to Cashlean—our spoil he said ; but it might be that he guessed you were not far away.— He thinks highly of you, David. He said that four times you had a man at your mercy, with danger around you, and did not strike to kill—and that once he was the man. But you must go now," she urged. " My mother is waiting for me at the next point, and I promised not to be long."

" She is a noble lady," said the priest, and taking Eithne's two hands he bent over them and drew close to whisper : " We three will meet again, my dear one. This is not the end."

CHAPTER XVIII

A WILD WELCOME HOME

BEFORE I finish this part of my narrative, I am impelled to say something of our home-coming to Dungiven. It was the first homecoming in all my life, the first time I realised that here was a home where I would be welcome for myself alone. Surely it was this knowledge that finally brought me into the fine fellowship of men.

It was on a still and sleepy afternoon that Senan and I rode up the glen to the brink of the ford below Dungiven. Our enduring small horses were spent and thin, and we draggled and weary. We had taken the full week on the hidden twisted road from Corrib, and most of the days and all of the nights had rained on us—a warm rain but a wetting one. That was the only discomfort that befell us. Our boots and cloaks were mired, our faces stubble-bearded, our eyes weary for undisturbed rest. My blackcock's tail was the only jaunty thing about us. And here at last was the haven of Dungiven ; and Dungiven, that grey old dún, seemed a castle of the dead. No one moved about it, no one moved in the township on its flank. It lay there, slumbering and aloof in the haze of heat and had no welcome for us. Not even a bird sang—and one bee went humming by sleepily. Our hearts went heavy in our breasts, and a great heaviness and lonesomeness came down on top of us.

" All of them," spoke up Senan bravely, " men, women, and children, will be down the strath haymaking, and the garrison having a sleep to itself—same as Ferdoragh above."

Ferdoragh, guard of the gate, sat on his stone by the dark of the arch, his head down on his breast and his lean shanks spread abroad. He did not hear our horses splash knee-deep across the ford, he did not hear the hooves on the causeway ; our shadows were on him before he lifted his head, stumbled hastily to his feet, and blinked rapidly. His mouth opened and shut with a click. "Great God be praised!" he cried. "Is it ye?"

"It is," said the priest bitterly. "And why would not I be cutting your goat's head off with the sparth?"

"God be praised!" cried Ferdoragh again, his eyes alight. "Is it not grand to hear you, and ye back to us again?"

"Are we the last?"

"And the long last. Ye are all home now. A house of the dead this was, instead of a wedding-house—and the chief going about blaming a holy friar—and his lovely one at the weeping. Go on in now, my darling fellows! Go on in now, and 'tis I will let them know the great day is in it."

We rode under the gloom of the arch, and he yelled after us, "Horo! the wedding-feast, and it lasting till Lady's Day."

And as we rode out into sunlight of the wide courtyard the great bell in the tower began to boom. Ferdoragh was leaping on the rope, and the brazen clang roared and roared.

That bell was only rung for a great feasting or a deadly alarm, and so it now waked the dún with a hum and a clamour. Out from the big living-house, from the penthouse, from shady corners men came tumbling, half-dressed and barefooted, grasping sparth or sword or spear—anything that had blow in it. And then they saw us, and the stark note of fierce alarm paused and broke queerly and changed into the high and terrible note of the slogan. That high peal with the note of triumph in it made my hair stand up. And the thudding boom of the bell was inside my head.

And all at once they came down on us in one mad rush, mouths open and arms tossing. Our horses reared·in panic, and I was in a panic too and stared round me for a refuge. Between a notch of the parapets above I saw Donal Ballagh's head turned down on us, and a red crown shining in the sun was at his shoulder. I swung Benmee for the door of the tower, but next instant I was lifted bodily out of the saddle and whirled here and there about the bailey. Great hands clapped me, strong arms clasped me, voices roared and laughed all around me. I saw old Turlough Mac an Teaclan with the tears running down on his white beard. Çalvagh MacManus shouted in my ear : " To-morrow we would be out at the searching—I needed you." Teig Ironhand, his mouth red in his black beard, roared heartily : " Now will my little one be happy."

Presently the press about us was shorn through impetuously and Donal Ballagh had an arm round each of us. His eyes were flaming in a white face, and he kept repeating as if to himself, " Well—well—well ! " Until suddenly he shouted, " Laggards ! Laggards ! You will pay for the fright on us."

My ribs bent under the crush of his grip and I threw an arm across his shoulder. He was my own blood-cousin and we liked each other. I felt a tightness in my throat and my eyes stung.

The bell had stopped booming now and quiet came suddenly ; I could feel the feet shuffling in the dust. The men made room about the three of us, and the lovely young wife Amy came through. Her blue eyes were swimming in tears and her mouth was quivering as she smiled on us. She caught the old priest's hands and kissed them, and faced me, a quick shyness in her look.

" There she is for you," said Donal, shoving me forward. " Will you salute her ? "

I tugged off my bonnet, bent knee, and lifted her fingers to my lips. And as I straightened up she placed her hands softly on my shoulders and kissed me on the rough cheek. " You are welcome home, cousin," she whispered. " We were so unhappy."

My face flamed to her flush, and I could scarcely let her hand go. That was the finest of our welcome. But the welcoming was not yet over.

Donal was again holding us and swung us towards the door

of the keep. "There are a couple of words to be said," he threatened. "Come this way."

At that old Turlough lifted his great voice.

"Justice!" he bawled. "The clan will have justice." Donal turned to him. "Who withholds it, bellower?"

"I warn you, Donal Ballagh O'Cahan. There might be good telling in this and the first of it is the clan's due. Ah! look at my old friend and the gleam in his eye."

"There is a tale surely," said the priest, clearing throat in anticipation, "and if we had a bite and a sup—— "

Behold us, then, sitting at the long table in the mid-house and a mood of high feasting all round us. I sat between Donal and his queen, with Senan at her other side, and the board was weighty before us and all down its length. Those who could not reach the table ate and drank standing, and all the time the turmoil grew. For the boom of the bell had roused to hurry all who had heard it. Men—old and young—working in the fields had grasped any weapon to hand and come in at the full stretch on pony or on foot; in couples and threes they streamed in, and as they arrived Ferdoragh shouted the news, and fresh cheers broke forth and a fresh press of welcome came about us.

There was a lump in my throat and the meat choked me, but I took two deep gulps of Garonne wine and that steadied me. Now I knew I was one of the clan and that the coming home of Senan and me had put the great finish to a great adventure.

CHAPTER XIX

A SUMMONS FROM RED HUGH O'DONNELL

DONAL BALLAGH O'CAHAN, Amy his wife, and myself leant on the ramparts of Dungiven and looked idly up the Glen of the Roe. The valley was a wealth of greens and browns, and the thin hot haze of autumn lay like a veil on the quiet face of it. The croon of the river came to us sleepily up the causeway; the warm air lulled us, heather-scented from the south ; peace lay on the broad of the world.

It was a month since my return to the dún. I found that Amy had made no high-handed essay to change the habits of the dún, but had set out to make a pleasant domain of her own that would woo man and maid to it. The great bailey with its penthouses and mid-house she left alone for the present. These were the men's quarters, and the men were grateful for not being disturbed. But at the west side of the dún where there was a postern she was already planning a terraced garden, and even now the masons were building the outer wall to it. " If this war comes," she said, " it will keep the old men and myself busy, and you will see green lawns and flowers and a lily pool where that packed clay is— and you will learn to tread gently and doff bonnet and practise fine manners."

" My fine fellow ! " cried Donal, turning to me, " your mother's portion is yours, and maybe you will be noticing how our uncle Conn over at Derry Columcille wants you to stay with him. He has two ships in the Spanish trade and no one for them. When will you try the merchanting ? "

" When you kick me out."

" A small while yet. But all the same, we three will spend a week with him soon. I would like a ship myself."

" We cannot," said I. " There are twenty men here to learn the arquebus." This same uncle Conn had brought us from Spain a score of a new-pattern weapon with an improved lock, and I was busy training the men to it.

I glanced along the white of the road that twisted west down the glen—and then "Look!" I said suddenly. "Mounted—— "

Donal turned quickly, palm above his eyes, and stared intently down the valley road. "From the O'Neill, think you?" he put to me quietly, but his feet shifted restlessly.

"From someone—and that hurry on him."

Donal looked down at his wife, and she, seeing the trouble in his eyes, pressed close to him. "Not yet," she whispered, half to herself. "The truce still holds."

We leant over the ramparts and watched the rider, a saffron-clad kern with spear hip-slung and heels in his horse's flanks. He was pressing his mount cruelly and would be at the ford in half a minute. Already we could hear the thud of unshod hooves and see the blurred shadows flit on the sun-baked road.

The rider splashed across the ford, and there came faintly the high challenge of Ferdoragh.

"We will wait here," said Donal quietly, holding his wife's arm. She gazed at him, and he smiled down at her. A steadfast man when the pinch came.

We had not long to wait. In a minute, strangely drawn out, we heard a shuffling on the stone stairs, and the red head of Calvagh MacManus rose into the frame of the turret doorway. "Rider from O'Donnell," he shouted, excitement in his voice.

The kern stumbled into the light and swayed on his feet. He was covered with dust; even his black glib* was powdered white; and his face was grey and haggard. Behind him came old Father Senan puffiing after the long spiral.

"O'Cahan?" inquired the man hoarsely, blinking from one to the other of us.

"At your service, friend," said Donal.

* Locks of hair hanging down over the forehead.

The kern saluted and cleared his throat, and Donal looked with reprimand at his foster-brother.

" He would take nothing till he said his word to you," Calvagh excused himself.

The man wetted his cracked lips with his tongue and began the speech that he must have committed to memory on the weary road. " Hugh Roe O'Donnell sends brother's greeting to O'Cahan and seeks his help."

" The Sassenach ? "

" The Sassenach—a red wind wither them ! Listen, chief. This is what I am to say : The great fighting-man Sir Conyers Clifford, with the loyalist dogs of Clanricard and O'Connor Roe, two nights ago came down on the fords of the Samhaoir and tried to storm the dún of Bellashanny. They failed that time but are in a ring around it, and Hugh Roe O'Donnell is gathering help from the four winds."

" Hugh Roe used to be strong enough to guard his own borders," growled Calvagh.

The kern stiffened. " Hugh Roe can do more than that as the world knows, but Clifford the wily one picked his time well—when the clans were in shieling and the dún with a bare garrison. Thirty standards of foot, ten squadrons of horse, a ship from Galway with engines landed to batter down the walls—and over against them in the dún a handful of bonnachts under Hugh Crawford out of Alban. Chief, I was bid say to you that this is no small foray. If Clifford wins Bellashanny he holds one gap of the north, and O'Cahan is no safer than O'Donnell. Hugh Roe asks your help. That is my word." He threw out his hands in a sudden sharp gesture and pulled himself up to hear the answer. And he got that answer on his last word.

" O'Donnell shall have O'Cahan's help," said Donal quietly.

" That was known, great O'Cahan," cried the messenger, and suddenly went limp. He staggered, and Calvagh put a holding hand on him.

" See to him, brother," ordered Donal. " He is of the true breed."

Calvagh and the O'Donnell clansman disappeared down the dark curve of the stairs, and we stood silent, listening to the shuffle of the feet on the stones. The young wife turned her head aside from her husband and looked across the ramparts at the brown side of the glen beyond the river.

Donal did not look at her. He stood up very straight and held her arm firmly within his. " It is on us—the big blow," he said, " and we must look to our plans."

" Your plans are made," said the priest.

" We have but decided to send help to Bellashanny. This is only the beginning. Remember O'Neill's warning ? De Burgh, Kildare, and the Pale will come down full force on Dungannon, and there the full brunt will be. That is what we must prepare for."

" Then your place is here," said Father Senan.

" Well ? "

" The thing to do is the thing I see in your mind."

" And it ? "

" Send all the horse you can spare to Bellashanny— with a good man to lead them."

" And who would that man be, I am wondering ? " Donal smiled, his eye away from me.

" There is a middling good man that I have in mind," said Senan.

The two laughed, but I saw nothing to laugh at in this serious business. I turned sullenly enough to Donal, and he clapped me on the shoulder. " David, brother ! Your two-score horse must be at the Samhaoir to-morrow, before nightfall. Your lead, with Calvagh as your second. What are you standing there for and time pressing ? "

I heard Amy's sigh of relief. Here was respite—and de Burgh might never strike. Alas ! In a week Dungannon became an armed camp with all roads leading to it.

CHAPTER XX

WITH O'DONNELL AT BELLASHANNY

THAT was a strenuous ride through a wild and lonely land. Our road led us across vast moors purple with heather where the lapwing flapped, calling warily, and the grey plover piped plaintively along the slopes ; by black tarns where bog-lilies floated and dry reeds shivered in the wind ; down into quiet valleys where small streams gurgled and corn-patches yellowed in the sun ; and up long stone-ribbed braes grown with yellow whins, that crackled in the autumn heat and breathed their mystic odour into the air.

The haze of the fall was over all the land ; there was a stale feel in the keening wind ; high in a pale sky the yellow-tinged clouds sluggishly drifted. It was like riding through the land of a dream.

And it was a land emptied of men. In the corn-fields women bent to the hook and stooked the sheaves ; in the wattled townships women came to the doors and watched us out of calm eyes ; in the upland shieling women herded the black kine. They spoke little to us riding through. Quiet they were as their own hills, patient as their dumb earth. " Bring our men home to us," cried one young woman. " Laggards, laggards ! " taunted an old hag.

But surely we did not tarry on that road. Our first night's camp was in a pine-wood near a hamlet with a stone dún, where the women brought us oat-cakes and curds, and an ancient shanachie, fighting done, hobbled to our fire and gabbled of old raids into Tyrone in the days of Shane. Before the fall of the second night we had reached the Samhaoir.

The wind blowing to us brought the hum of the siege long before we sighted it, and told us that we were still in time. Every four or five minutes the deep thunder of the culverins shook the air, and, in between, a rattle of arquebus crackled and spat. And at last, topping a slope, we saw the dust and smoke lift and roll, and yonder across a mile of plain was the stubborn dún of Bellashanny standing above the Falls of Assaroe. It was dim in the pother of dust, and to the right smoke rolled up where the culverins thundered on the breast of a round hill. On that hill we could distinguish the straggling lines of an entrenched camp, and on the plain below a yet larger camp—a huge camp this, curving from the river and ringing hill and dún. The Samhaoir lay below us like a carelessly dropped ribbon, with wimpled stretches where the fords were, and at each ford were armed men.

" Let us down to it," cried Calvagh eagerly at my side.

" Down with us then ! Twos in good order."

But we were already late for any of that day's merry work. The fight sallies were dying with the sun and the culverins were now silent, while the smoke-cloud slowly lifted and rolled away.

We rode straight for the camp, keeping the curve of the river on our left and making a string to its bow. Midway on the string the guards at one of the fords saw our array, and a single horsman galloped across to us.

" Young Maguire," shouted Calvagh riding up from the rear. " See the yellow mane to him."

It was indeed Doncadh Donn Maguire, my gay lad of Dungannon : bareheaded, with a hawk's feather in his splendid hair and a black corselet carelessly buckled at the shoulders. At first he did not know me. " Ye come late," he shouted. " From where ? "

" Dungiven," I called back.

" O'Cahan's lads ! Ah and is it David Gordon, by the high powers ? Blackcock's Feather ! Oh-ho for it ! And there is Calvagh himself." He galloped and swerved to my side, eye and hand welcoming. " And where is Donal Ballagh ? " he inquired.

" Waiting word from O'Neill."

" Same as my father. Once on a day Donal could not be held from a rally like this."

" Two-score of his best here," said Calvagh.

" To be sure ! You will be wanting to report to Hugh Roe ? "

" If we find him."

" My camp is yonder by the ford, and an ox roasting. Send your men across. They know my lads—they were all at Clontibret together. I know where O'Donnell has his quarters near the Abbey, and we two will ride over to him."

It would have suited me fine to ride up to Red Hugh, forty trained men at my back, but here was the wise and kindly word, so I swallowed my vanity and gave Calvagh his orders.

Maguire and I backed away and watched the men swing off in rank. " Work you put into those heroes," he commended. " Let us on."

" Fine talker," said I, " have you any word of this siege ? "

" A hundred thousand ! Faith ! there are two sieges and hot as hell on Easter Monday : the Sassenach at the dún, and we at the Sassenach. Clifford the fox in a trap of his own setting ! Friday, in the night, he sallied up from Sligo, surprised the fords at the dawn, and hoped to surprise the dún. But my bold Crawford, Hugh the Albanach— you met him at Dungannon—jerked the drawbridge in his face and settled down like a badger, every tooth with a bite to it. So siege it had to be—or retreat, and tough Clifford took his chance. He planned the game neat as a bout of chess, but foolish to make plans and forget how Hugh Roe O'Donnell might tumble the board. And that is what Hugh did. Not waiting to marshal the clan he swooped down with the men he had handy, beaconed all the hills from here to Innishowen, struck here and struck there like a flash, and struck harder as his strength grew. In tens and twenties

came his clan, angry as the red bees, and from over the
border the Maguires, the O'Ruarcs—and now yourself. By
noon, Monday, he had forty companies on the Sassenach
flanks, and yon is how we have them now."

He gestured wildly from river to castle, and I envied
him his fine roll of words.

" On Saturday the Sassenach held all the fords as far
as Devenish, now he holds only one—the Path-of-the-Heroes
above the falls—and he has a collar-and-elbow grip on that
his only road. My lads behind won the ford we hold—
a bonny fight—to our waists in water and hitting overhand,
and when a man went under he stayed under. To-morrow,
and God is good, we will put the Sassenach in the trap and
the *gabhlóg** down. The Sassenach ! Ay, and all the royalist
dogs of Connacht—O'Connor Roe, Clanricard, and his
son Rickard the Sassenach. Is it true you cut out Rickard's
tongue ? "

" It is not. Can Crawford hold the dún ? "

" That fellow ! Tough Hugh ! with eighty Scots bonnachts
and ten days' food ! That badger will not be drawn.—We
turn right here—Hugh Roe will be down by the Abbey."

The sun was behind the high square tower of the dún
that stood out black and sharp against a warm sky. The
smoke had blown away, the rival camps had ceased their
worrying, and instead of gun-peal and slogan a great and
peaceful hum rose from plain and hill. The Irish camp
that we skirted was a medley of hastily erected shelters, and
it was as full and busy as a hive. Here and there fanned
fires began to flame cheerily, little spirals of smoke twisted,
and groups of men were busy round the cooking-pits.

" A hard and merry day," said Maguire. " That smell
makes me hungry. Let us hurry. Siege and counter, attack
and sortie, skirmish of horse and struggle of pike—from
dawn to dusk. We were not strong enough to carry their tren-
ches by open assault, and the dún defied them in spite of their

* Forked stick supporting a trap for catching birds.

arts. They battered at it with their culverin, tried to set a mine in the arch, made essay to bridge the moat ! Blazes ! but you should have seen the mailed fellows tumble in the ditch when Crawford set their wooden tower afire. Yon now are O'Donnell's quarters."

We had swung round the north edge of the camp to where the Abbey of Assaroe looked across at Innis Samhaoir. Between the Abbey and the island we could see the clean green of the sea, golden tracked by the sun, with an anchored ship swinging black against the gold.

" There is Hugh himself," said Maguire. " The young lad with the red hair. The small fellow is O'Gallagher of the Gallowglasses, and the big black lad MacSweeney of the Axes."

O'Donnell's quarters were in the stone guest-house of the Abbey, but the young eagle stayed outside in the open air. With the two notable chiefs named he sat on a bench before the door, looking out along the track of the sun. Our approach made him turn his head, and seeing us he lifted to his feet.

I looked at him with interest, for this man's fame was overseas. I knew he was not old in years, but I had expected him to be war-hardened and grim. And he was only a lad : a young, lithe, shapely lad, with finely-red hair, a delicately smooth face, and grey wide-set eyes. He looked at me and then I knew the force that was in him. For his eyes had the hooded-eagle set under the wide brow, and he had a way of leaning forward from the hips like an eagle ready to swoop —and aye ready was he. " Is it you, Donn ? " he called, high and clear. " Keep you a tight grip yonder ? "

" A double hold, Hugh, with forty men just in from O'Cahan. This is Donal's cousin, David Gordon, who leads."

O'Donnell looked at me with quick interest. " You are welcome, David Gordon," he said. " Your name is known. My mother—God rest her—was a Scot too."

" A sword hand to him by all accounts," said O'Gallagher, who had remained seated, one knee across the other.

" Horse or foot ? " inquired O'Donnell.

" Horse, O'Donnell," I replied.

" Drilled men too," amplified Maguire ; " half of them with flint-lock."

The young leader's eyes lit up, and it was only when they lit that one knew how the Gaelic gloom lay behind them. " It is kindly thought of the O'Cahan," he said warmly. " Horse we need. You will camp with Maguire for the night. To-morrow the fight will be for the Path-of-the-Heroes, and your horse will have good share in it. Luck with ye."

We rode back to the river by the skirt of the camp, where the fires were now bright and the men at food, and splashed across the ford to where our men were settled amidst clumps of willows. My lads were already at home amongst the clansmen of Maguire, and as noisy around the cooking-fires as the owners of them. There was talk and laughter everywhere, as was the way of these Irish fighting-men.

With Calvagh and Teig Ironhand I looked over the horses. They had been watered and well picketed amongst the willows, and the men had found a trampled corn-field and had cut the heads off the ripe corn for a fine pile of forage. And then Donn Maguire, Calvagh and I sat on our cloaks by the brink of the Samhaoir, ate roast ox, and talked of the morrow.

Twilight was darkening round us, the camp-fires far and wide twinkled brighter, a drone as of bees drifted with the lazy air ; behind us a gallowglass laughed, at our feet the river gurgled. Overhead the sky was high and deep, with little grey cloud-islands floating amongst the faint stars ; a great peace folded us in ; we seemed to be far and far removed from war and death ; we stopped talking of battle and its chances. Then the day's long ride came home to me and I yawned.

" Bless me ! " cried Donn Maguire, " I forgot.   Let

us be taking a fine sleep to ourselves, in the name of
God."

I pulled my new mail shirt over my head and lay on my
back, folded in war-cloak, but sleep did not come to me
for yet awhile. I stared into the deepening blue between
the stars and thought of many things. Now at last was I
soldier and leading my squadron of horse ; and men, who
were good men, talked of me as Blackcock's Feather. And
luck was coming my way. For with the Sassenach and the
loyalists trapped on the Samhaoir, Connacht was open to us,
and the great O'Donnell would not hesitate in sweeping it
from end to end. And what then ?—what then ?—And so
I drifted into sleep.

CHAPTER XXI

THE RUNNING FIGHT FROM ASSAROE TO SLIGO

MY awakening was desperately rude. A hand gripped
my shoulder and bit, and Donn Maguire's voice shouted
in my ear.

" Gordon ! David ! The fight is on."

The daze of sleep on me, I caught his hand fiercely. " What
is it ? "

" Listen to that ! " His hand tugged at mine and lifted
me to my feet, cloak about my knees.

I shook my head as if the turmoil was in it and looked
towards the dún. Down there red flashes cut across the
dark, arquebuses cracked, fierce yells ran through the night.

" A sally on the camp," cried Maguire.

" The Ford of Assaroe ! " I exclaimed.

" Never the Path-of-the-Heroes in the dark ? " cried
Calvagh, who was at my shoulder. " Let us get the men
horsed," he bellowed in my ear.

There followed a nerve-dragging time of blind feeling

for straps and buckles, of the shouting and movement of men, the tugging and rearing of startled horses, and a scrambling and pushing into some kind of order. When at last with shirt of mail settled on my shoulders and sword in hand, I sat on Benmee a-quiver at Maguire's side facing the ford, I drew a long breath of relief. The horse were arrayed behind us in double line, and the gallowglasses crouched fully armed amongst the sallies at either hand.

The night had changed while we slept. A clouded sky hung over us ; big drops of rain spattered now and then on my mailed shoulders ; the air was thick and hot. Yet the night was not dead black, for somewhere southwards the moonlight suffused greyly through the cloud-pall and showed us the waters wimpling with uncanny gurglings down the ford.

"A finger for a blink of light ! " cried Maguire. " It is hotter down below."

It was, though the arquebuses no longer crackled. Steel clanged, men shouted, events were afoot ; and we at the ford, not knowing what to do, waited for the issue. We had not long to wait. A horseman came clattering out of the dark beyond the ford and racketed to a standstill at the edge of the water.

" Dogs ! Dogs ! " he yelled. "Are ye up ? "

" Who rides ? " thundered Maguire.

" O'Donnell's word. To the ford—to Assaroe." Frenzy must be swaying him in the saddle. " The Sassenach are crossing. Down on them and hold them till the clan musters. Up with ye ! " He swerved his horse away and was gone up the river towards the fords of Devenish.

" It is so then, David Gordon," said Donn Maguire, suddenly calm. " Let us down and push them over Assaroe."

The gallowglasses came breaking through the sallies. I manoeuvred my men out into the open, behind the clumps, and with Calvagh and Teig keeping touch on the wings, we pressed forward on that desperate venture.

The English without doubt were making good their escape from the trap. Sir Conyers Clifford, hardy man of war, was playing dice with death—a bold game boldly played. North side of Samhaoir was failure and death, south of it the bare chance of getting his force behind the distant walls of Sligo. And he took that chance to save his men and his province. Leaving guns and stores as spoil, he, in the heart of the night, marshalled his men down to Assaroe, and squadron by squadron marched them shoulder-locked through the rush of waters above the falls—the Ford-of-the-Heroes, and every man a hero that night. Behind their leaders—O'Connor Roe, Clanrickard, Dunkellin, Vaughan, Cosby, Wingfield— they marched in good order, and if here and there a man lost his feet, the thunder of the falls drowned his last cry. Half, two-thirds were safe across, when a Scots sentinel on an outwork of the dún caught the glimmer of moving steel in a vanishing ray of moonlight and guessed its import. His alarm roused the garrison who lit a bonfire on the ramparts and themselves sallied out, firing their arque-buses.

O'Donnell, roused out of sleep, did all he could, but he could never hope to array his wide-flung clan in time to bring the enemy to bay. The more eager of his men, half-clad from their sleep, grasped sparth and spear and came yelling their slogans on the English rear. But they came too late, charging on a stubborn rear-guard all steel and buff, that took minutes to die and gave the main force time to marshal its columns on the left bank and begin its orderly retreat. O'Donnell's men, dammed back by that stubborn rearguard, flowed upstream to the next ford, and with this scattered body our gallowglasses intermingled as they blundered along in the dark. Calvagh, Teig and I kept our lads out on the flank of this jumble.

I have never met any man who could tell clearly the story of that night. All that any man can say is that there never was the like of that running fight from Samhaoir to the gates of Sligo. It was one long-drawn-out rallying and worrying of maddened men in the dark.

The English foot kept in close column, hugging the sea ; the English horse, split into squadrons, flickered around it front and rear. They were fighting for life and no better fight was ever made. Time and again the clans gathered force and stormed down on that massive column ; time and again they were met doggedly by hedge of steel ; time and again a squadron of horse stemmed those yelling rushes, were surrounded as with a flood and drove a way through—a remnant, captain and trooper knee to knee. Men died, and dying were trampled under foot ; riderless horses bucketed out of the press ; yells of hate and rage, triumph and challenge, rent the night ; steel rang on steel, thudded dully on buff, went silent through warm flesh. But that iron column, rallying and mending its rents, held doggedly on its way. And at long last came the pale dawn stealing, and over there in the distance were the towered walls of Sligo.

I, who led them, will say that my forty men did their share that night. My post as leader steadied me, and until the very end I was not concerned with my own part in the fight. Once I mind a pike striking on my mailed shirt and nearly lifting me out of the saddle ; once I was in a staggering *mêlée* on the brow of a cliff and heard the waves boom between the shouts ; and once I exchanged blows with a halberdier knee-deep in the tide. But my whole mind was bent on nursing and still nursing my troop, and using it cannily where we had a chance to do our share. No foolish attempt did we make to stem a charge of the heavy Sassenach horse. Twice indeed we charged on a broken remnant and emptied many a saddle, but mostly we skirmished across the front of the column to our light and hardy horses and tried to retard the retreat. Time and again, avoiding the full charge, we swooped out of the dark slantwise at the head of the column, forced it to set itself in a pike-hedge, and swept by just outside the points. When the final rally came

I still had thirty men behind me, but by then our horses could hardly raise a trot. Calvagh was still with me, but Teig had been dismounted somewhere in the dark.

Dawn came and saw us surging against the walls of Sligo. We had failed to hold or break the enemy. His dead were strewn along the coast, his horse were only a remnant, but still he faced us as stubborn as ever. And Sligo was now ready to receive and save him—and save Connacht.

It has been argued that if Sligo had been a mile farther away none of the English force would have escaped. It could be well. O'Donnell's men, scattered from Devenish to the sea, had not been ready for a night attack, and eagle though Hugh Roe was he necessarily took a long time to get his heavy-armed gallowglasses into action. All night long away in the rear he had been mustering his scattered men and sending them forward, but it was only now in the dawn that he with his main force came down on the English flank. He was too late. With Sligo walls in front he had no room to swing forward and cut the enemy off. But even so, he very nearly succeeded in winning Sligo.

The east port was open ; the portcullis had creaked up ; the head of the Sassenach column was pressing through the arch when O'Donnell made his last desperate effort. And this time my men charged home with the clans. The remnant of Clifford's horse tried to stem us, but we flooded round them and one by one they were dragged down to death. And there too—sad day !—I lost my great mare Benmee. A big pikeman, teeth a-grin, thrust her through the breast and she sank under me. If my feet had been in stirrup nothing could have saved me. As I was falling forward under the pike of the soldier a fierce grip pulled me to my feet, and there was the great foam-flecked beard of Teig Iron-hand at my shoulder. At once the press was round us and we were only two units in the storm.

We bore down shoulder linked on the Sassenach rear and drove in with it to the gate. The rear broke and we

intermingled with it, still striving forward. That was a tense
minute—Gael and Sassenach in one swaying mass—hacking
sideways and yelling into each other's faces. We reached the
gateway. Nothing could stay us. Already a score or more
of us were in the gloom of the archway and then !—Then
the portcullis clanked down, pinned a halberdier as if he
were a fly, and snapped that press of men in two. Half
a standard of Sassenach were left to die without, and our
score were trapped in the arch.

I was one of that score.

CHAPTER XXII

THE COMBATS ON THE TURRET STAIRS

A MINUTE ago I was one of four thousand harrying a
beaten enemy, now I was one of a score trapped and doomed.
For yet a minute I did not realise it. Then above the din a
voice cried in my ear. " We are in it now." It was Calvagh
MacManus at my shoulder.

" And hard dying," boomed a voice at my other shoulder,
and there was the flaring beard and bloodshot eyes of Teig
Ironhand.

And as I twisted head to look back at the massive grill
of the portcullis there was Doncadh Donn Maguire, his
back against the bars, his golden hair a-toss and his eyes
gleaming. Why not ? We four had been in the front of that
last charge, and we were big enough and strong enough to
keep our places.

" Let us kill," roared a big gallowglass of the Maguires,
his voice high above the worrying of the clans dammed
against the portcullis.

But there was little space there to kill or be killed. Our
score, mostly together, faced inward. What few of the enemy
were amongst us were already dead and held upright only

by the pressure. I stood breast to breast with a tall halberdier whose weapon was broken above the axe, and by the grin in his teeth I knew he was the man that had killed Benmee. " Dog ! " he cried in my face. " If I had a hand free——"

With a sudden side-thrust of the shoulder he made an inch of room and jerked his halberd-arm out of the crush. " I have you now." But at that a look of shocked surprise came into his face and his lifted weapon fell behind his shoulder. " You've done for me," he whispered and his face twisted.

It was Teig. At the small of my waist he had driven his great hand forward, and his *scian* had gone home.

It was not pleasant to see the man die. I strained back and let him slip to the ground, and his room gave my sword-arm room—" Let us die in the open."

And we had our way. For the first time that night the English broke before us. They were safe within their walls and now they did not want to die. They turned and strove inwards and we drove them. And when they reached the open, they did not at once wheel round on us, but scurried away right and left, and gave us an open space below the big gate-tower. In a little time they would rally and turn and then the end would not be long. That great cobbled space was crowded with men, and beyond them was a street of wooden-joisted houses running downhill into a grey sky behind the grey roofs.

But we did not die just yet. We were a panting clump of men just outside the arch, and suddenly Doncadh Donn Maguire with a great shout whirled me round. " Look ! " he cried.

The tower north of the gate was buttressed by a dozen stone steps, and at the head of the steps was a wide-open door. No doubt the tower was garrisoned and the portcullis room full of soldiers, but here was a chance we could not lose.

" Up ! Up ! Up with you ! " roared Maguire, bundling the nearest man forward.

" Let me die in the open, chief," prayed desperately one of his own gallowglasses.

" Like a wolf! Be badger now, Uilic, and sell your life dearly."

As we made for the steps, the nerve of the Sassenach returned. A yelp, as from a pack, and their long front surged on us.

" Steady, brothers, steady ! " It was Calvagh, cool as at drill. ·" Two at a time and we are all in."

At the head of the steps Donn and I turned at bay. Leaping at the head of the English was a big fellow in fluted half-armour, a sword in his hand. Back through the night my arm had ached from gripping hilt, but now I felt no ache as I brought blade up and went down a step.

" Here is the weapon for him," cried Donn. " Leave him to me."

Maguire had broken his sword sometime in the night and was now armed with the long-handled axe—the terrible weapon of the gallowglass. The big fellow came leaping up at us. " Have at you ! " he cried. And Donn swung his axe. That was all : the big fellow crumpled and rolled down under the feet of his men.

Donn yelled clear and high, threw up his axe, and next moment I had him by the belt and through the doorway. Calvagh banged the door shut, and Teig shot the big bar into its slot as the weight from outside burst against it. The tough oak strained and held.

The room we were in was the main guardroom but we did not pause to examine it. Every man there had only one thought—the portcullis chamber above our heads. If we could win that before the walls of Sligo were manned and lift the portcullis, Sligo might still be ours. The men were already at the turret stairs and crushing upwards on each other's heels. There was no hanging back for these fine fellows in that crisis of death.

And, alas ! death it was. Maguire and I were not half-way

up the dark curve of the stairs before the fight broke out above us. The portcullis chamber was fully manned and here was our last fight.

It was a great window-slitted chamber covering the whole floor of the tower, and there was plenty of sword-room. The heavy top-bar of the portcullis stood six inches out of the floor, and there was the heart of the fight. Though the guard outnumbered us, our first charge swept them across the room, and Calvagh got the holding-pin free and two men in the chains before they rallied and charged back. And this time reinforcements came pouring in to them. For another stair led up from the south tower, and by this, the soldiers came and came and came.

I was no rat in a trap. I was not sorry for myself. I surely was not unhappy. If I could describe my feelings at all, I would call it exultation. I was no longer the silent, dour Scot. I laughed, I rallied the men cheerfully, I shouted; and oh ! but I was deadly. I was tall, with great shoulders and strong wrist, and I moved lightly on long legs. I used the point mostly, and I knew that my father, if he could know, would not call me clumsy. No man could withstand me that day. The power came from somewhere inside myself. Men faced me and parried, and I drove right through them. I raged in a fine gaiety across the floor and back, and the men followed and died round me—but the end was certain.

There we were, now, at the foot of the next flight of the turret stairs—all that was left of us.

" Up to the next floor," I roared. " We can hold them there. On, Maguire ! "

Up we struggled, Maguire and big Uilic supporting Teig, who had been wounded. Calvagh had been struck down, not by a Sassenach, but by a traitor gallowglass of Clanricard's who had got home with his *scian* below my comrade's guard. We were now in a low-arched sleeping-room with a four-poster bed in one corner and tapestries on the wall. Through the window-slit I caught a glimpse of a hill far away, and the young sun made a glow behind it. It seemed a glimpse of another world.

Teig Ironhand was my man and I took him in my arms across to the couch, while the others watched the stairs.

He had a clean cut slantwise across the thigh, and I tried to staunch the bleeding. There is one thing that every clansman takes to war : a pouch of dry moss—the same healing moss which the great Dalcassians made use of to staunch their wounds that time they fought their way home from Clontarf. I applied a great pad of this and bound it with strips torn from the couch covering.

" Small use now," he whispered, and as I bent over him he touched my shoulder with his great hand. " You led us well, Gordon ! " he said. " We were your children. The clan will know." And after a pause : " Pity this is the end for you."

" Not yet, brother," said I.

" No. It would be fine to die under the sky." He turned his head to where the light came through the window-slit.

" We will do that," I told him.

Again I took him in my arms, and went across to where a curtain hid the last up-flight of stone steps. " Let us to the open," I called to Donn, leaning like a cat at the stairhead.

" That will be best," he agreed, after a pause.

" This is the place for me while I have a tooth left," said big Uilic.

" Stay and kill then," said Donn, his hand against my back on the stairs.

Up on the battlements we drew clean breath once more. I laid Teig down in a corner by the turret tower and straightened up. The smooth flags of the roof spread before us a score of paces—a square floor shut in with notched parapets and roofed by the sky—and the clean wind of morning blew across it and stirred life in us afresh.

With Donn I leaned against the open door, looking down

into the gloom of the twisted stair. Down there, where had been so much turmoil, was no sound at all now. No sound at all for a long time, and then a great voice roared, " Here is for you, dead man."

The thunderous bang of a petronel shut on the last word and the crash of a fall followed. Then came a sudden clamour and a voice of authority broke out above it. " Back ! Back ! Some are still above." Ensued a scuffling and growling and clank of arms against stone.

" And there went Uilic Mor," said Donn. " Our turn now."

But our turn was long in coming. Everything was again still. Without a word I turned and strode across to the parapet and looked away from it to the plain below, and there were the clans drawing off from the fight. They were in complete disarray and mounted men galloped across their rear, urging them away out of gunshot. And who, I wondered dully, was to gather what was left of my two-score horsemen ? It did not matter. I was only fifty feet above them, but all life lay between us. Never now would I ride at their head again. Never now—never now——.

Donn Maguire's low whistle called me and I walked across to his side. He held his great axe ready and looked at me out of wild deadly eyes. " They come," he whispered. " Listen."

I heard nothing. I laid my hand on his arm. " Donn," I said, " let the last rally be here in the open."

I drew him back from the doorway and willingly he came. " Let it be so, long man," he murmured, oddly resigned.

The man who came, came quietly, and we let him come. Almost before we knew, his morioned head appeared out of the dark spiral. It stayed moveless there looking at us.

" Come on," I cried. " Two at a time and no quarter."

At that he came up and stood still in the doorway. And he was Sir Francis Vaughan.

But a very different Sir Francis Vaughan. No courtier

this. This man was haggard and grim and strong—and very cool ; his eyes steady in black-rimmed deep sockets, grim battle writ all over him. He carried broadsword in one hand and petronel in the other. I was sorry that I had to fight this man.

He thrust petronel in belt and dropped the point of his sword. "Enough killing," he said quietly. "You are my prisoners."

" Never—never," cried Donn Maguire hoarsely, throwing up the axe. " I will never surrender to hang in a Sassenach gibbet."

" David Gordon," said Vaughan, " tell your friend that you are my prisoners and will be honourably treated."

Maguire looked wildly at me and I held his arm.

"A man of finest honour, Donn," I told him.

And Donn drew his hand across his eyes.

CHAPTER XXIII

PRISONERS OF WAR

MAGUIRE and I had confidently looked forward to an escape on the march down from Sligo to Athenry, but Vaughan had kept us under such strict guard, that we never got the faintest chance. Teig Ironhand, with his wound, had been bestowed by Vaughan in a safe place in Sligo out of Dunkellin's reach, and of Teig no word had reached us, though we learned later that he had made good his escape.

The half-town of Athenry was a medley of stone, wood and wattled houses, straggling within four stone walls and garrisoned by four Sassenach standards, as well as by some clan levies from Dunkellin and Clanricard. The road from Athlone came in below the castle at one side, and the road to Galway ran out between barbicans at the other. It was the main loyalist stronghold south of Cong, but its Governor,

Sir Francis Vaughan, had few good words to say of its security.

" This fort of Athenry," said he, " is proof against attack on all sides save that on which we look for it ; this sunken north wall would tempt a beldam to launch a sally at it."

He, Donn Maguire and I were leaning on the shelter-parapet, looking across the pasture grounds to the distant woods.

" But I know that if I face O'Donnell again," Vaughan went on, " you will see me with an advance guard, a rear guard, a strong reserve, and an open road behind."

" We will not see any of these things, jailer," put in Donn, laughing ruefully. " You keep the devil's own grip on us."

And that was plain truth. We had now been three weeks in Athenry, and Vaughan's grip was surer then ever. He had treated us fairly and very wisely. He had taken us down to the dungeons of the keep and chosen the best one for us, one of the few that had light from outside. It had a stone floor and stone walls and a stone arch for a roof, an iron-clamped door and a barred slit of window level with the fosse. And outside the door was a dark stone passage and stone steps leading up to the main guard, with another strong door at the head of them. " You are dangerous men," he told us, " and I will hold you with might and main ! "

" Perdition ! but you will," said Donn sadly, looking round him in the grey light.

" You can have these quarters," went on Vaughan, " or you can pass me word of honour."

" What is that ? " asked Donn eagerly.

" It is this, and I pray you to accept it ; plight me word that for one week you will not seek to escape, and at the end of that time renew it if you see fit. Meantime, you will have full freedom within Athenry, and without the walls if accompanied by me or an officer deputed."

" My fine hero ! " cried Donn heartily. " I plight my honour this minute."

It was the only thing to do at that time. There was no

hope yet of an invasion out of the north, and there would be no heroism in immuring ourselves in a stone cell. And now for three weeks we had renewed our word and we had nothing whereof to complain. Sir Francis was doubly kind. Wishful to give us as much freedom as was possible, he did not quarter us in the castle, where the hours were disciplined, but lodged us in a wooden-joisted house below his doubtful north wall. In this he showed his trust, for in the rear of the house was a drying green sloping up to the glacis,* and to escape, any dark night, we had only to risk a ten-foot drop into the dry ditch. In these quarters we were wholly free and our landlady, a woman out of Wales, widow of a camp-surgeon, was careful of our needs and our comfort.

Doncadh Donn Maguire, always gay of heart, was enjoying life to the full, and indeed but for a certain irk of mind, I too had no cause to complain. Donn's father, the great old Hugh Maguire was ever a stern and serious man and had never yielded anything but reprimand and restraint to his son's levity of spirit, but now the lad was free though I kept some sort of hold on him, and he found congenial companions amongst the garrison officers. These were of the new train-bands, young fellows all, not yet soured by war, coming mostly from the wide country of Devon, and thus in habit of mind and pursuit of sport, very kin to the Irish without the Pale. Donn knew the English tongue and had been to England in O'Neill's train, and so was at home amongst them. He was to be found in their quarters most of his waking hours. He threw them at dice; he matched them at rapier foil; borrowed a horse and went hunting and racing with them; bought, borrowed or stole a gamecock of high breed and fought mains all over south Galway as far as the Clare passes; and went with them to the parties occasionally given by the few ladies in the garrison.

I was of the quieter breed and not made for easy friend-ships. That ugly-set face of mine was against it, as well as

* Bank sloping down from fort, on which attackers are exposed to fire.

the reputation that rumour had falsely tied on me. The young fellows shied away and held me in something like awe. Some of them had seen the quarrel in the " Pied Horse " in Dublin ; and had heard exaggeratedly of the raid on Rickard the Sassenach ; two or three had been at the harrying of myself and Father Senan at Corrib ; and the fight in Sligo gate-tower was known to all. None of these adventures, one might say, was of my own seeking or habit ; I no more than happened to be drawn into them and chance had centred on me and on my blackcock's feather. Belike it was this unique plume that called attention to me and gave me a dangerous name.

Though Donn Maguire was of my own age, he never treated me as such. Rather was I the gruff, but not too difficult uncle. He confided in me, never took my advice, made fun of me in his gay way, and looked to me to get him out of small scrapes. He borrowed and spent the last of my coins, and then through the agency of the Galway merchants, raised credit in his father's name and came to me clinking a full purse. Whereupon I laid him on his back, took it away from him, and doled him out coins painfully when his need grew clamorous.

With only two of the English officers was I actually on easy terms. One was Vaughan himself, a sterling man who improved on acquaintance. He had seen life in camp and court and could sail in all winds. A keen satiric man, veiling a strong core. My habit was to visit him in the castle in the forenoon, take a cup of wine with him, and listen to his talk of three Courts—wild tales sometimes ; and on occasion he visited us in our quarters.

The other was Ned Billing, captain of the north gate, a ruddy grizzle-headed veteran, very fond of a dry French wine, and an expert in the chase. He had spent so many years in Connacht that he was grown Irish in habit and very largely in sympathy. He was one of the few English that spoke Gaelic fluently. " Old am I for changing," he told me,

" and stiff in the bone for night work, or with Wat Tyrrell I might be." This Walter Tyrrell was an Englishman, and a very notable leader of forays on the Irish side.

Ned was indeed a great lover of the chase and had himself bred two fine hounds named Satan and Urith Ban. He knew every covert from Suck to Oranmore and was not guiltless of running another man's stag—as I found out in our expeditions into Dunkellin woods.

An old acquaintance in the garrison was Tom Pybus, Vaughan's body-servant. A queer dumb fellow this big trooper. Here in Athenry he had always avoided me, and if ever I caught his pale blue eye, there was something sheepish and abashed in it. That I could understand. I had treated him roughly and something contemptuously, and no soldier could forget such treatment.

CHAPTER XXIV

DEFEAT AND DEATH OF THE LORD DEPUTY

ONE evening Vaughan came to see us in our quarters. He was wearing military dress, and his face was set to hide his thoughts. I pulled a chair in for him without a word, and he sat, his arms on the board, while Donn filled out a stoup of wine and moved it before him.

He took it and smiled to us. " Your good health, my enemies ! " he said and emptied it at a draught.

" Bad news, Sir Francis ? " I put to him, for we had been hearing rumours.

" Bad news, indeed." His voice was quiet. " But good news you would call it, and you may. Your O'Neill and O'Donnell have given us another lesson in strategy and a double stroke to drive it home."

Across the table I saw the light leap in Maguire's eyes and his yellow mane seemed to lift. Yet he said no word and did no more than move the flagon in front of Vaughan.

Vaughan helped himself and looked at me. " You are eager to know ? "

" What you are pleased to tell."

" Not pleased, my friends. But I will tell you. You are aware that the Lord Deputy's design was to strike from Connacht and through the Gap-of-the-North by Armagh. You know what befell the first stroke—and the second was no luckier. At the very beginning young Trimblestown and a thousand men were cut to pieces at a bog-pass in Upper Meath by Tyrrell and O'Connor."

" That is the way the two have," murmured Donn.

" But the main attack on O'Neill was under de Burgh himself. He rebuilt the fort of Portmore and tried to wile O'Neill into the open out of his strong places round Dungannon. O'Neill gave wile for wile. He kept his main force masked and set his horse and light-armed men to watch and harry the Queen's forces. Both leaders were playing for time : O'Neill waiting to hear from O'Donnell before risking open fight, and de Burgh waiting for Clifford's flanking movement before he drove O'Neill into the trap. And then came Clifford's failure and O'Donnell with a picked force came hastening to his ally. After that, there was no more biding time. De Burgh found himself face to face for the first time with heavy-armed soldiers—gallowglasses you call them—and men trained to the arquebus. Twice he essayed fight and twice was he beaten ; and now the remnants of his force are scattered from Dundalk to Dublin, and Portmore is close beleagured by the North. That is the tale."

" It was great fighting," said Donn, a muscle twitching in his cheek. He was holding himself in very well.

" The North has given us a big debt to repay," said Vaughan. " But there is something that cannot be restored to us. William de Burgh, who was husband to my sister, was sore wounded at Drumfliuch, and this day lies under the sod at Armagh."

" It is good to die in war," said Donn. " God rest him." "Amen," said I.

" He was a good soldier," said Vaughan, " and honest—no courtier, but believed men as they spoke. A malison on the ruffling boasters of Dublin ! They made him belittle his enemy, and stayed safe within walls while he went out to die."

A silence followed. We all sat thinking our own thoughts and these in time came to the same groove.

" I am sorry," said Vaughan, " but I must hold you."

" The devil's tight hold too," said Donn chagrinedly.

" I fear that a dull time is before you—but, belike, a right lively one for us. Clifford is taking no risks. He assumes that O'Donnell will make a descent on Connacht before winter. If he breaks the Sligo line, there is nothing to hold him between there and here, and it is here that we shall hold him—Galway, Athlone, Athenry. I pray God that he will venture so far."

" If Hugh Roe comes," said Donn slowly, " you will maybe not thank God for answering your prayer."

Vaughan laughed for the first time. "At least we shall welcome him warmly," he said, and turned to me. " Cong and Tuam are being abandoned and we are to be strengthened by the Cong garrison." He looked from one to the other of us. " I can trust you two soldiers not to quarrel with the new men ? "

" Faith, no ! " Donn promised. " If the clans come south of Cong we will take to your dungeon and bribe your jailer."

He nodded understanding. " Until then I pray you to leave things as they are. There is no need to immure yourselves within walls, for I assure you that escape is impossible."

We left it at that until Vaughan had taken his departure.

And then Donn got up suddenly and paced up and down the room. " That dungeon ! " he exclaimed ; " that dungeon ! It is like a stone coffin to get out of."

" One of us inside and the other outside "—I suggested.

" By the great wind ! A bright thought ! My fine man ! You could be getting down to the ditch and pulling a bar out of the grid."

" The grid is too narrow. A friendly fellow like you might bribe a jailer on the outside."

" The best way to bribe one of these is to clout him over the sconce, and devil the hardier fellow than yourself——"

"And my head on a pike a short time after."

And all that evening we discussed and rediscussed half in play, half in earnest, our chances of escape. In the end we decided that if O'Donnell came south of the Cong line, one of us would lodge in the dungeon, while the other from the outside must seek by guile or force to effect a rescue.

" Vaughan is wise and wily," said Donn doubtfully, and will see what is in our mind. Like enough he will pop you in to keep me company."

And so the discussion circled round once more.

CHAPTER XXV

MEETINGS OF FRIENDS AND ENEMIES

IT was on a dank afternoon in October when the reinforcements from Cong arrived.

At the time I happened to be alone on the sunken north wall in the rear of our quarters. There was a moist feel in the air and a thin mist hung low over the sweep of plain that I could see beyond the head of the slope outside the wall. I was gazing idly over the grey level, dotted with kine and here and there a spear-armed herdsman on a rough garran, when the long line of the Cong garrison crawled out of the woods on to the north road ; first a troop of horse, then a column of foot, a disorderly array of townspeople, a medley of ox-drawn wagons, a park of culverin, one behind the other, more ordered foot, and the rear brought up by another troop of horse. They crawled slowly across the plain, and I watched with some interest until the bastion hid them from my eyes. Then I went down to my quarters and, in tune with the dull weather, speculated dispiritedly on the future.

We were doomed to be prisoners within these walls for how long? A throw of dice, a main of cocks, a scraping of foils—boys' playthings! A little hunting, it might be, but no adventuring to Galway. Nothing but idling amongst soldierly enemies, with a careful watch on tongue and manner, while Sir Francis prepared a warm reception for our friends. Was there nothing we could do? Nothing!

Donn was slow in getting back from his usual visit to the castle, and I think I dozed for a while and dreamt that I was deep underground with someone knocking over my head.

It was Tom Pybus at the door. It was evening then and I was hungry. " Sir Francis begs your presence at the castle, sir," he told me.

" Was that the Cong garrison? "

" Yes, master, and Cong town with it."

I thought I understood Vaughan's message. He wanted me to meet Cosby in his presence, and make sure that no sword-work would ensue. There was no danger of that now—on my part—but Vaughan had better have his surety. I donned my best tunic, smoothed out my blackcock's feather, left sword and *scian* behind, and followed Pybus. As I slanted through the square at the heart of the town, the Cong garrison was taking up quarters in the wooden shelters that Vaughan had hastily built for it.

There was a group of officers round the peat and bog-pine fire in the great hall of the castle—some, my acquaintances of the garrison, others of the newly arrived force—and the scullions were laying the table for supper as I strode towards the turret stairs.

I pulled aside the curtain at the stairhead and stepped into the upper hall. It was finely lit with new heavy waxen candles and the tapestry stirred gently in some draught of air. About the cavernous fireplace were scattered fully a score of people, men and ladies. Donn Maguire was there for sure, and Vaughan, and big Cosby with his upright head and light hair, and talking to him a tall dame whose back was turned.

And facing me down the length of the hall was Eithne O'Flaherty.

I stopped for a single instant and my heart gave an empty leap. And then my feet took me up the hall. There was nothing else they could do. Easy now, easy, David Gordon ! Your ugly hatchet face is a fine shield and many eyes will be looking at you. Take your cap in your hand and you will be getting through this somehow.

I walked directly to Vaughan. " Your pleasure, Governor ? " said I.

" You were slow in coming, David," he greeted me with easy familiarity.

The tall dame turned. She was a noble-looking lady— with long chin, and long nose, and strong deep eyes under the brow.

" Captain Dame Bevinda O'Flaherty," introduced Vaughan, " let me present David Gordon."

Her eyes held mine and she gave me her hand frankly.

"Ah ! Blackcock's Feather," she said, and smiled. " Connacht has heard of you and Connacht has been unkind to you."

" Not always, Dame," said I, bowing deeply.

"And this is the Lady Eithne," went on Vaughan.

Alas ! we were far away from the Glen of the Echo and the mood that was easy on us then. Our eyes met. She curtsied and I bowed. That was all. But while there was a flush of warmth on her cheeks, there was an odd transparent pallor as of excitement about her mouth, and her dark eyes shone deeply under the lovely dark curve of her brows.

Vaughan put his hand on my arm and kept it there. " Captain Cosby," he said, " this is my friend David Gordon."

We stood up to our full heights and looked at each other. He was tall as I was, and his eyes that used to be bosses of pale stone were now yellow like a lion's. This was my enemy. More than that, I was his deadly enemy. Vaughan was wise in bringing us together in this company, for if I had met Cosby anywhere else, my hand would have sought hilt at a whisper.

"I have met Captain Cosby," said I and could not bend my stiff neck.

"And will again by the devil's grace," he said in his strong voice, his head upright and his neck like a pillar below his powerful jaw.

"Which side his majesty?" said Vaughan. And then quickly, "But let that be, gentlemen."

"At your service, Governor," said Cosby. "He is your prisoner."

He turned his shoulder to me and spoke to Eithne, and I saw her shoulders lift in a long breath of relief.

Dame Bevinda was now speaking to Vaughan. It seemed that he had placed his upper chambers at the disposal of the Dame and her party, and she was insisting that they must keep the disciplined hours of the castle. She asked him the supper-hour, and he told her seven of the clock. "A proper time," she commented. "If we might, we will go to my woman Breadh till then." She turned to me again and smiled. "There will be great talking between you and me, Master Gordon."

Vaughan and Cosby accompanied them to the turret stairs. Eithne gave me one quick look and one quick smile, and that was all. No word had passed between us that used to talk so freely. A great strangeness had come down upon us, and our old mood seemed gone beyond recalling.

I was alone on the floor and here and there curious eyes were on me. I looked round for Donn. There he was under a wall-light, Ned Billing and himself making talk and laugh with a bonny fair-haired woman. I went towards them.

Donn caught my arm. " Lady Duvesa MacTheobald," he introduced. And to the lady, " This is David Gordon of the blackcock's feather you wanted to meet, Lady Duvesa."

The lady's merry grey black-lashed eyes went over me closely, and I hoped that having had their fill of my dour face they would need no more. " I am glad to meet the great David Gordon," she said in her silver tinkling voice. "All Connacht speaks of him and his feather."

" He did his share," said Donn, " when he was well watched."

Then the bugle went for supper and there was a movement towards the great hall. Bold Donn edged off with his Duvesa, and left Billing and me to follow in the ruck.

We found a seat well below the salt, and Ned hunched over a great round of beef and carved for both of us. " One good thing," said he, " this alarm of war has given us the pick of the beeves of Hy-Many—besides the ladies."

" Beef for me."

" I saw you being presented to the lovely Eithne."

" You know her ? "

" Know her ! With all Connacht I respect the mother and love the daughter. Though bluff Cosby has the pull of me there." He looked up the table and grew serious. " The shame of hell to see her wasted on that boor ! I suspect the mother. A wise lady, that Bevinda, for all her boldness. Note you that she draws no steel in this war. Your Red Hugh in his swoops gets no stable hold on Connacht, and until he does, she leans to the power that leaves Cashlean-na-Kirka an unburned roof. But she is Irish at heart, and not ill-pleased to see us Sassenach get our full of hard knocks. You will be knowing why she chose Athenry instead of Galway as winter quarters ? "

" I do not."

" Because Cosby is here. The maid and he are plighted, and the wedding is to be here on All Saints'."

So that was it.

Supper over, I went across the square where a big campfire blazed before the wooded shielings, and down East Lane to our quarters below the north wall. In the drying-green at our rear the voice of Donn hailed me. "There's a man in the house looking for you," he said.

The man I saw leaning on the table in the wavering light of the candle within our room was Cathal O'Dwyer of the Glens. "You are welcome, Cathal O'Dwyer," I greeted him.

"Am I, David Gordon?" he asked, wistfully, his face a-quiver.

"My friend! my own brother! Rest you. This is Doncadh Donn Maguire of Fermanagh."

"Namely son of a namely father—Breastplate of the North," acknowledged Cathal.

"And a heart in him harder than the breastplate," said Donn.

In the Glen of the Echo, Cathal recovering from his wound had been in weakly health; but now that his wound was healed, a more terrible blight had fallen on him. He was thin and haggard, his shoulders fallen in and an angry red flush high up on his cheek-bones.

"Is Garrodh here with you?" I asked him.

"He is not. I came in with the O'Flaherty tail."

"And your lodging?"

He hesitated. "The kerns are kind."

"But I, your brother, should be kinder. There is an airy attic up under the roof, and out in our green you will get all the sun that is going."

He demurred faintly and I kept patting his shoulder. I was woefully grieved for this my friend. There was a terrible fatal light in his eyes that I could have wept to see. Indeed, he was near tears himself and his face quivered. Donn poured him out a fine mether of wine and he drank it slowly and daintily. And then Donn, with an excuse, left us. He knew O'Dwyer's story.

"God is good," said O'Dwyer. "The fine friends one meets when the need is the sorest—finer than I deserve."

" What you deserve from me," I comforted him, " is everything. You and your foster-brother, God rest him, set my feet on a man's road."

"And it brought you here ? "

"And will lead again from here. And here too, there may be work for me."

He looked at me closely. " There may be surely." He threw his hands wide. " But look at me," he said, " and the strength gone from me—a blast on me—and my work undone."

" Is it still on you ? "

" I cannot help it. Mark you, David Gordon, it is easy enough to kill Cosby the Killer. A throw of spear or pull of bow and it is done. But I want to see him face to face and see the knowledge of doom in his eyes. And I am only a withered branch—a withered branch." He looked long at me. " I know," he said. " I know. I will not put it on you, my friend."

I looked on the ground and spoke between my teeth. " Whatever you put on me," I said, " I will do it in the face of the world."

" Then I can rest," he said.

And I knew if Cosby killed this man, I would pursue Cosby to the gates of hell.

Next morning after breakfast I took Cathal into the drying-green, where the sun was warm ; and there I left him wrapped in his long cloak. When I got back to our room, Donn Maguire had disappeared. Myself slung on shoulder-sash and, instead of Andrea Ferrara, thrust black *scian* at hip. Carefully I brushed bonnet and re-set feather, and throwing short day-cloak on shoulder, made my way towards the castle where the renewal of my word was due to the Governor.

Crossing the square, I saw Cosby directing the completion of the wooden shelters for his men. He saw me too and strutted across boldly, his basnet jauntily set on his upright

head. He faced in front of me and I had perforce to halt.
" Gordon," said he, his face cold stone, " we are ill friends
and will remain so."

" Ill friends, no ! " said I. " I am your enemy."

He sneered his cheerless grin. " My enemy ! A rebel
hired fighting-man ! If Sir Francis Vaughan who governs
here had not forbidden it, I might show you how we chastise
rebels. But there is one warning I will give you : presume
not on your acquaintance with the Lady Eithne O'Flaherty."

" I am on my way to thank her," said I, " for once saving
my life."

His eyes yellowed. " You had better move carefully."

" I will be very careful," said I.

For a moment he forbore my eye and then, swinging on his
heel, stalked away.

The great hall of the castle was empty, except for the
halberdmen on guard. The sergeant told me that the
Governor was in the town, and, on this, I ventured to the
upper private hall, where I found a middle-aged tire-woman
building birch logs about a new-lit fire. She was a stranger
to me.

"A terrible thing," said I into the air, " to waste the fine
morning at the sleeping."

" Is that the way, tall young hero ? " said she, merrily
aware of my meaning. " The young ones are about this
hour and more, and maybe could be found for the looking."

" I came to see the Governor," I told her, " and will wait
for him on the east wall."

" It is a good place to be at the waiting, surely," said she
pleasantly.

At the left of the hall was a door giving on the east wall, a
favourite exercise ground of Vaughan's and mine. I lifted
the latch and stepped out, and there was Eithne herself,
strolling down towards the bastion at the corner. She was
not alone. Duvesa MacTheobald was with her, and on that
maiden's left hand, on the edge of the glacis, strutted the

bold Doncadh Donn Maguire. Their backs were to me, and
I was minded to slink back within the doorway before they
turned. But I hesitated too long, and they swung round at
the corner and saw me. So I walked up the wall with something of the pikeman in my parade. And, with a pang,
memory recalled the quiet Glen of the Echo, and the days I
used to go down to meet a maid at Echo-point.

It was a rare morning, with a high clear sky full of austere
autumn sun, and a clean breeze out of the west. And this
young lass, walking straight and lissome in the sun, with a
black curl blown across her brow, was born of the sun and the
wind. She welcomed me with a smile, a warm, somehow
half-shy, half-mocking smile, her head a little bent and her
eyes looking at me from under her bent brows. Donn and
his lady welcomed me too, but not so much for my company
as for my convenience.

" I was telling the ladies," Donn cried, " that this was our
favourite stroll of a morning, and that we would maybe not
permit them to share it."

It was Vaughan's and my exercise-ground, not Donn's, but
I let it go.

" This morning we will take, then," cried Eithne. Frankly
she came to me and took my arm. " I want to talk to you,
David Gordon," she said. " Be off, young ones ! "

CHAPTER XXVI

BLACKCOCK'S FEATHER WITHDRAWS HIS PAROLE

AND so, in couples, we walked the east wall from castle to
bastion and back again. Below, the glacis sloped to the open
space behind a street of low houses ; at her shoulder was the
parapeted shelter-wall, and beyond it the grey-green plain
spreading to the woods, with smoke from the shieling fires
blowing across it and mounted kerns driving cattle to the
grazing.

"And now, David Gordon," she said, " you will tell me everything about Dungiven and my darling Amy, wife of your cousin."

" She is very happy."

"And her husband at war ? "

" Then she may be sad too."

" Tell me about her. How does she carry herself? "

" She is very kind and very wise."

" Go on, please ! What is she doing in that place of men ? "

" She is creating her own domain—building a sunken garden, with a fish pond and a lily pond, and a walk of the box tree."

"And does she ever speak of one poor Eithne O'Flaherty ? "

"At great length. Of her impish ways and her engagement—and her great ferocity."

" But she, indeed, might. Oh ! but I would love to see her and see her happy ! "

"And she would like that lady to visit her in her garden when it blooms," said I.

" Said she so ? That would delight me." She let go my arm and clapped her hands, happiness in her voice.

" Yet I think that you will never visit that garden in bloom," said I, who could not let her be happy.

" Why do you think that ? " she cried quickly, a little startle in her eyes.

" You will be very far away."

She threw up her head and looked at me. " That is a poor reason—that is a poor reason." There was pain in her voice, and then she was calm again and spoke even-toned. " If Amy asks me I will come—even if I be far away."

" You will be welcome," said I.

"And I wonder who will welcome me ? " And then she was silent, which was strange, for never had I known this maid to be lacking in speech. We met Donn and his fair-haired Duvesa once, twice, before another word passed between us, and then she changed the subject. " How is my old priest ? "

" Well. And is not done speaking of your splendid goodness."

" Goodness, no ! Happiness, yes ! Was I not a queen then ? "

" With your wise man—and your fool." Why was I so bitter ?

" But we were happy."

" Surely. It were churlish to regret folly."

" Oh ! " she cried. " Were you the foolish one ? "

" Who else, lady ? "

" Why, I was beginning to think that I—but never mind. Since we are at Corrib, let us go on. You got home safely ? "

" We did."

"And you came back to Samhaoir leading a troop of horse ? "

"A troop of bonny men."

"And lost them in Sligo tower ? "

" Left most of them outside—alive, I hope."

"And twenty of you held the gate-tower against odds ? "

" For a little only."

" They speak of a man who was more terrible than Conal Cearnach or Cuchulainn. He wore a bonnet with a black-cock's feather. And he came a prisoner to Athenry. Men say that a man like that man could not be kept behind stone walls unless the walls suited him—for a reason."

This was hitting with bare steel.

" He was but a plain soldier—and foolish," said I.

" Still foolish."

" Still the same folly, my lady.—Here is one, now, that is no fool."

"And there speaks folly. But I like your first folly best." She laughed, not unhappily now.

Cosby came striding along and stopped before us, his light insolent eyes on me. " Said your thanks ? " he inquired shortly.

" They will keep till tomorrow," said I carelessly.

" Eithne ! " he cried, " If this prisoner is importunate, a word to me or Sir Francis——"

She laughed merrily. " David Gordon," she said, " was most entertaining, and I look forward to tomorrow." She looked at me with smiling eyes.

" I shall not be lonely any more—but I was."

" At your service, lady." I lifted bonnet and marched by Cosby, my shoulder stiffened in case he barred the way. But he forbode that push.

Within the hall I came face to face with Captain Dame Bevinda. She smiled at me, and then shook her head. " You have been taking the air with my daughter, David Gordon ? " she said bluntly.

" I have, Dame,"

" Was that wise, stubborn man ? "

" It was not, Dame."

" You know she is wedding Sir William Cosby at All Saints' ? "

" It is said, Dame."

"And I say it now. Let me advise you for your good. But why ? You will go your own gait, I know, but where will it lead you ? "

" Where it will, Dame."

She looked at me steadily under her brows—her daughter's very look. " I wonder what you would dare, David Gordon," she half-mused. "Ah ! daring is easy for men such as you, but men such as you are never sure how much to dare. Can you read that, Blackcock's Feather ? "

" I will think it over, Dame."

" Do that, then, David Gordon." And she turned and left me.

In the bailey of the castle I met Vaughan hurrying in from his defences. " You are in haste," said he.

" And you too, Lord Governor."

He laughed his light laugh. " To perdition with dull

duty ! I was hasting to pay my respects to a darkly-fair damosel. Hast seen her this morning ? "

" On the east wall."

" Lucky rogue ! " Then he grew serious. "Art aware that her marriage with Cosby is set for All Saints' ? You are. Then what is to be done about it ? "

"Ask Captain the Dame that."

" Rather would I ask the daughter. I fear that she is wasted on our Cosby, and I would venture the guess that she knows it. If I help to spoil Cosby's sport I look to you to do your part. Where is he now ? "

" With her on the east wall."

" Then here goes, spoil-sport," he cried, and hurried away.

Donn Maguire overtook me at the square, and thrust his arm within mine. " You will listen to a few words from me, shut-mouth," he said.

" These four weeks——"

" You never told me you knew Eithne O'Flaherty."

" Nothing to tell."

" No ? Tell me now. For a fortnight you saw her every day ? "

" Ten days only."

" But you two became great friends ? "

" Well ? "

" And it might be a little more ? "

" You forget long Cosby."

" I do not. Duvesa MacTheobald——"

" Let us speak of that one."

" I like her," said Donn simply, and very seriously.

" A small saying for you."

" Just that. But wait you ! Duvesa thinks—she more than thinks—that this affair with Cosby is of the mother's planning, and that if you——"

" A kind clan of busybodies you all are," I stopped him sourly.

" To the mischief with you, then ! " he cried hotly, and
threw my arm away.

But I caught his arm back.

" My dear David ! " he cried warmly. " Would I not
give my right hand to help ? "

" We are prisoners here, and can do nothing."

" Something must be done. Take you to the dungeon,
and O'Dwyer and I will get you out of it in spite of all.
Remember you are cousin to Donal Ballagh, and what
he did——"

But I was set in a hard mood, and stopped him. " When
O'Donnell gets south of Cong you or I will take to that
dungeon. Let the rest be."

Whereon Donn abused me fluently.

I will not chronicle closely the smooth-running course
of the next eight or ten days. They were uneventful days
in Athenry, but from outside it, away up north, news of
stirring happenings came thick and fast.

For O'Donnell donned his eagle wings, swooped down
on Clifford's northern line, and smashed it utterly. Sligo
fell, and the O'Connor Roe was sore punished for his English
leanings ; Ballymote was abandoned ; Boyle surrendered ;
Tulsk was burned to the ground ; and the clans rolled south
gathering strength as they came. The MacFirbis, the
O'Dowds, the MacWilliams, the O'Haras, the MacDonaghs,
the O'Kellys, the MacDermott, the O'Costello threw off
the loyalist yoke and flocked to the northern standard.
Nothing could withstand that advance, and any day now
Cong and Tuam might be occupied.

Donn and I waited the word, and no word came. Suddenly all news of the advance ceased. It was as if the clans
had sunk into the ground. They might have swerved east
to Athlone or west to Galway, or, for all we know, marched
back with their immense booty to the Samhaoir.

Athenry was full as a hive with the loyalist refugees pouring
in to the safety of its walls. Clanricard and Dunkellin in our

rear were marshalling their unwilling clans ; Clifford at Athlone wrote urgently to Ormonde for reinforcements ; Bingham of Galway hurried Londonwards on like business ; and Vaughan, bent on holding Athenry, strengthened his north wall with half a score of culverin, filled his granaries, and salted down his beeves. Nothwithstanding many a lesson, the English forgot that the Eagle of the North seldom came the expected road. They were but circling themselves for another onfall.

Donn and I now held ourselves aloof from the garrison and the loyalist lordlings. We looked on these latter as traitors to the blood that ran in them, and that view of ours they sensed and were bitter about. We owed it to Vaughan to take no part in bickerings, and if we sought the crowded company in the castle there is no doubt but the hot-headed Maguire would have blade out of scabbard before a day.

With Dame Bevinda I became strangely friendly, and I often sat with her in the upper hall and talked of many things. For some reason I could not fathom, she showed a liking for my company and my dour short answers, and I liked her straightforwardness and her steadfast purpose.

All Saints' was due to fall on a Saturday. Came Monday of that week and a great hunt. Under Dame Bevinda's and Cosby's arranging everything seemed to be in good train for the wedding, and already the great hall and the upper hall were being decked for the feast.

We were at supper that evening in our room—Donn, Cathal O'Dwyer and I. The landlady had come in with cold pasty and light ale, and I turned to the table, though appetite was very far away from me.

" Supper, Donn ? " said I.

" To the pit of hell with you and your supper ! " he roared at that. And for all of five minutes he used every insulting word he could remember in Gaelic and English, and they were many. Cathal stared from one to the other of us, dismay in his face that we two should have come to this pass.

At last Donn quieted down and, with sudden resolution, came to the other side of the table and leaned across to me. " What are you going to do, full-mouth ? "

There was nothing in my mouth but a slow tongue.

My silence set him off again. " Oh, Great Michael's sword ! Look at him, O'Dwyer, and All Saints' on top of us ! I will be spitted by the devil's prong before a maid like that one is wedded to a Sassenach shield-striker.— —What are you going to do ? I asked you ! It would be finer of you to think of the woe that will come to an Irish maiden. Well ? " he queried fiercely.

" Heaven knows, Maguire, you are right," I cried. " To-morrow my sword goes back to Vaughan."

"And as I love my mother ! " vowed Donn, " if we fail to get you out of your stone coffin in four days I will break word myself and snatch Eithne O'Flaherty to a safe place." He straightened up and ran his fingers through his yellow mane. "Angus of the Birds ! " he said cheerfully. " I got that done more easily than I expected. Fine man, reach me that pasty and I will be trying your share and mine."

Donn Maguire had me up with the sun next morning and, after a hurried breakfast, helped me on with mail shirt and sword-sash. Cathal O'Dwyer came down from his attic to see us go, and smiled gravely out of his wasted face.

" We will meet again, brother," I promised, my arm on him.

" If God is kind, friend of my heart," he murmured quietly.

And we did meet once again.

In the great hall of the castle the halberdmen were already at morning duty, and at the head of it near a new wood fire Sir Francis Vaughan sat with a thigh over a corner of the table and waited for his morning drink. As we strode up to him he looked at me and my war-dress curiously. " Will you try a broth of hotch-potch with me ? " he invited pleasantly.

I slipped off shoulder-sash and laid the great scabbarded sword beside him on the table. He quietly placed his hand on it. " Has it come then ? " he said gravely. " You withdraw your word ? "

" I do, Sir Francis."

" If you must, you must," He turned to Donn, his eyes narrowing contemplatively. " And you, Maguire ? "

" One fool at a time is enough," said Donn, cheerfully.

Vaughan smiled cynically. " Hold it not in your mind that I am that fool."

" The sorry day for me," said Donn.

For a space Vaughan looked musingly on the floor, his hand on my sword, and a toe-point tapping quietly on the flags. At the end he drew a long breath.

" Let it be," he said. " We cannot suffer you to escape—and I will not." He called down the hall to his sergeant and gave him his orders. One man was sent for the warden, two set to guard me, the others to guard the door. He was taking no risks.

And then Donn spoke up in a careless tone : " I think I will see the lad into his cage—if you do not mind, my Governor ? "

" Not in the least, Maguire," said Vaughan ironically ; " but set you one foot inside the outer dungeon door and within it you will stay. Please yourself."

" I will do that," cried Donn, " and it will be to take myself off lest worse befall me." He came and clasped my hand, and his bold eye flashed into mine. " Good luck with you, Gordon—and life to Erin O ! " And with a brisk salute he swung on his heel and marched high and proud out into the day.

The warden, an old key-weighted man, came and led us down the hall and through the arch into the mainguard at the other side. At the far end of this he unlocked a heavy door and led down a steep flight of stone steps to a grey lighted cold-smelling passage running right and left. I had been here before. But the door the warden now unlocked was not the door of the dungeon we had seen that time, but one at the opposite end of the passage. My friend the enemy was taking every care to hold me.

My guards stepped back to let me through and Vaughan followed me in. He pulled the door to behind him and we were alone in a low wide cell with a damp stone floor, a groined stone roof, and walls sweating cold from every stone ; it was dim-lit by a horizontal slit in the far wall ; I saw a three-legged stool overturned on the floor, a wooden stretcher on squat trestles against the wall, and nothing more—except a black rat that scurried as we entered.

" It is the best I can offer," said Vaughan. " I am sorry it is not better."

" Wide enough and high enough—and strong enough. What more ? "

" I am indeed grieved, my friend, grieved to be compelled to this. I would give a hand——"

" There is mine for you," I stopped him. " You are a true man."

We grasped hands firmly, and without another word he turned and left me.

The door shut, the lock grated, bolts shot home, and at last I was a prisoner within four walls.

CHAPTER XXVII

THE HONEST ENGLISH TROOPER REPAYS HIS DEBT.

I SAT on the three-legged stool and looked round me, but I had already seen all there was to see. So I put elbows on knees, head between hands, and, hunched up on that low seat, gazed down on the stone flags for a long time. I contemplated the slowing down of life, the terrible immobility that man must breed within himself to go on existing in a dungeon, concentrating all his mind down to a single point, subduing his thoughts to one level above nothingness; becoming so little the medium of sensation, drawing so little out of his store, that like the tortoise he lives to an extremity of years. Would I too learn that woeful art of doling out the thin stuff of life ? Time enough might be mine to acquire it. Four days ! and Vaughan watchful. Four weeks—four months—four—I prayed to God Almighty ! no !

I started to my feet—the three-legged stool fell over— and began a-pacing of my domain : six paces from door to window-slit and five across. Standing on tiptoe I could touch the point of the groined roof ; the door was steel-clamped black oak ; the window-slit was chin-high and barely a span wide, and the mortar binding the cut stones that framed it was iron hard. By looking at a certain angle I could see a narrow band of sky above the tip of the fosse, but on that day the sky was greyly drear, and though I watched a long time there was never a rift of blue or gleam of sun to reward me.

That day was Tuesday. It passed slowly but not yet draggingly, for there was much to think about and one or two things to avoid dwelling on. Food in plenty was brought me from Vaughan's own table, as well as a couple of skins for night covering. Two tall halberdiers of the guard were my warders. One stood fully armed at the door while the other attended to my wants, and they made no attempt to open discourse with me. I was adjudged a man of desperate daring, for no good reason and the rumour of my name and deeds had grown foolishly monstrous.

Slowly the light drained out of my cell, and I followed it to the window-slit and watched the sad darkening of the sky. When I turned away at last I looked into black darkness that yet seemed to flow in waves and the rats were getting bold. With an effort I refrained from stamping foot and hissing them still, for I knew that I must grow accustomed to the pattering sound of these light feet.

For a time I sat on the edge of the trestle-bed hoping that someone would visit me. But no one came. There was only the dark, with the feet of the rats and the sough of a rising wind down the gut of the fosse. So I pulled off my steel over-shirt and lay down under the skins, hoping that sleep would come. But sleep, that fickle one, stood off from me, and thoughts that had been at bay all day broke in and would not be denied. What I feared to contemplate was the failure of rescue, the failure of O'Donnell, the long winter in this house of stone, and the gradual sinking into the lethargy that alone makes slow confinement bearable. And these I contemplated now.

Patience, David Gordon ! Be not a child fearing the dark and the cold and the rats. Give your friends—your splendid and leal friends—a chance to show their worth. In these you have been lucky. Your friends are busy ; they are bold and eager. Give them a little time. Nothing can happen this night nor, it may be, to-morrow night ; but on the third night—surely on the third night ?—some plan will be desperately evolved and desperately put to the test. For that you must be prepared in thew and brain. Be patient, then, and say your prayers—and sleep will come. And in time sleep came.

I did not sleep long—an hour—it could not be two hours.

It was the slow grate of the lock that waked me. I lifted to an elbow and looked at the door, and there was a faint gleam of light through the keyhole. A pause then, and the bolts were slowly levered back and the hinges squeaked shrilly. I saw a lanthorn in the opening and the big bulk of a man above it. The bulk slipped through and the door shut behind it.

" Who is it ? " I had one knee drawn up and my weight balanced.

He fumbled at the lanthorn door and the light diffused itself through the cell. The man was Tom Pybus. I sank back on my elbow.

" From the Governor ? "

He hesitated, and then, " No, master—my own business and yours."

I again stiffened elbow. Here was an East Saxon, man of a tribe I did not ken. What things might touch him deeply was a mystery to the Gael in me. To outward seeming he was quiet and stolid, stupid rather than placid ; but it could be that fires of resentment burned deep down in him. Three times in the past I might have killed him, yet did not ; but his life had been spared with something of a contempt that must rankle bitterly—and rankling bitterly——? In the hooded light I could not read his face, but in his hand he carried what looked like a sword. I was watchful. This fellow in handgrips would be as strong as a bull.

" Sit," I invited. " The stool is there."

" No master. There is hurry." But hurry or none, he was slow to begin and I could not help him. " Master," he said at last, " you have a great name as a swordsman."

" The name only."

" More. I saw you fight in Sligo gate and you killed men like flies. But look ! Three times you had me and let me go. Why ? "

He asked the question simply, and frankly I had to answer. " You were too easy to kill. Do you resent it ? "

" How ? You were in danger and took time to be merciful. That is what I remember, master—my life three times."

Here was a surprising Tom Pybus. Suddenly he sat down on the stool, shuffled his feet, and made a great effort to be articulate to himself and to me. " I am only a common soldier, but I am not blind to—to the things that be going on. Master, this be no affair of war or soldiering, and fair play is what I like—and you cannot have that behind a locked door. Master, whether I be doing right or wrong, I am doing what I must. I bring back your sword. Here ! " And there was the hilt thrust into my hand and my fingers curling round the familiar grip. " You will know what to do with it," he said meaningly.

Without another word he grasped his lanthorn and made for the door. I heard it close softly behind him, and waited, ears on the stretch. Silence only. There was no sound of lock or bolt.

I lay there for a time remaking my notions of this plain soldier, who grasped fair play as he saw it and was not troubled by any other loyalties. He had given me my sword, left me with an open door, and put the rest of the problem into my own keeping. " Do what you like now," he might have said, " and if it is not adequate your name belies you." Here was Finn's fair play and a challenge at the same time. It behoved me to stir myself and take all the risks that lay within the walls of Athenry.

I did not don my mail-shirt, since the weight of it might slow me, but slipped sash over shoulder, folded cloak over arm, drew my sword, and moved in the dark towards the door. I groped and found it, and it yielded to my touch with a long protesting squeak. I looked into the blackness of the passage and listened. Not a sound but my own blood in my ears. Even the rats were quiet.

On tiptoe I moved across the passage till I touched the other wall, and then, right arm advanced, went forward step by step till my shoulder, that had been touching the dark stones, slipped into vacancy. Here was the well of the stairs, and again I paused looking up into the darkness. The stairhead door into the mainguard was evidently shut. I felt with a foot for the bottom tread of the stairs, found it, and my back to the side wall, sidled upwards. One—two— six—ten stone steps and my outstretched sword-point touched the wood of the door above me. Slight though that touch was it set the door moving noiselessly, and before I might crouch I was looking up the long length of the guardroom. I drew in a long breath and sank down until my eyes were just above the level of the threshold.

CHAPTER XXVIII

A DARING ESCAPE

THERE was little to see, and everything there was to see at the same time. Just the dim-lit length of the great room and a group of soldiers round a rough table by the fireside at the far end ; and all but one of the group were bent over the board engaged in throwing dice with the death-and-life interest of the gambler. The man standing upright was Tom Pybus, his broad back to me and his hands clasped easily behind him. Directly above the table an earthenware lamp hung at the end of a chain, and this with the red glow of the peats was the only light in the room. Where I crouched was but the faintest glimmer.

The wavering smoke-tipped light gleamed on the angles of hard and eager faces, shadows sprawled and leaped as men bent forward to count the throws, and the outlines of legs were picked out to the last curve against the glow of the fire on the hearth.

I had to get out of that room. There were two doors to choose between. One was the door into the bailey, full

in the light of the hanging lamp, and I knew that a sentinel
walked the stone platform outside it. The other was directly
behind the dicers, but instead of wooden door it was hung
with a heavy curtain. Within that curtain, I knew, was a
twist of stair leading up to the armoury and to the portcullis
pent* beyond, and from the portcullis pent a short flight
of steps led down to the upper hall, which gave in the east
wall by a side door. There was my road.

I followed that road in my mind's eye and, as I did so,
big Tom Pybus moved a pace to the right so that his broad
back was between the dicers and the curtain. Here was the
plain hint. I looked across the floor. It was clear of impedi-
ment or scatter of rushes. Would I crawl on my knees or
slink along by the wall? I did neither. I walked slowly and
on tiptoe, holding my breath, and ready at a lift of head to
bound into action and drive a way through. And as I walked
I heard the dicers talk and growl and laugh. They were
baiting one man out of luck, and he was not hiding his
chagrin.

I moved the curtain softly aside from the jamb and slipped
through, and as the curtain settled behind me a bench
fell over with a startling clang. I had been seen! Now
for action.

I clambered up the wind of the stairs, no longer moving
quietly, bruised a shoulder against the pillar of the spiral,
and bundled, through another curtain at the stairhead—
straight into the arms of a soldier who carried a tallow dip
alight above his head. I had forgotten the night guard on
the portcullis.

The curtain had swayed into his face and he had not
yet had time to recognise me, but if his eyes were slow his
tongue was not. " Hog! What joke is this? "

My sword must have missed him only by a touch. The
hilt was against his ribs. My left arm was folded in my
cloak, but my hand was free and, as he grappled me, I

* Penthouse, shed.

drove clenched fist fiercely below his breast-bone. The grunt he gave was the last gasp of his driven wind, the lighted dip fell behind him, and he sank down between my knees and rolled over. I strode over him—and paused.

No steps came clambering on the turret stairs; from there came only the distant sound of voices and laughter. Then I understood. The unlucky gambler, tired of ill-luck and baiting, had only started up from the table—and started me hurrying. A lucky chance. Otherwise I must have met this fellow, now kicking on the flags, on mid-stairs and at a grave disadvantage.

Strangely enough the light had not been put out by its fall. It shivered, a faint glow, in some current of air across the flags, and I picked it up hastily, cupping it in my hand against the draught. The man on the floor was now on his back and I peered into his face. It was horribly twisted and his eyes were white balls. When his wind came back to him I must be well out of his reach.

Facing me in the steel-cumbered wall of the armoury was the door to the portcullis pent. I strode to it and up four short steps into a long and narrow chamber. The heavy top-bar of the grid ran along the floor, the windlass was at my hand, chains ran up into the darkness, and a cold air came up from below, and had a smell of the outside. At the other end of the chamber was mate of the door I stood within, and I made my way along the portcullis bar, drew the bolt and looked down a straight flight of stone steps to a heavy black curtain.

I crushed out the taper under heel, and darkness closed in on me, but at the foot of the steps there was a chink of light at the side of the curtain. I felt my way down, widened the chink carefully with one finger, peeped through—and straightway forgot the danger behind me.

There was the upper hall. The wall lights were not burning, but a branch of three waxen candles was alight on a small table near the fireplace. The arras was decked with laurel

6

and holly and the polished leaves glistened in the candle gleam. A room decked for the wedding-feast ! And yonder the bride. Eithne O'Flaherty sat at the table-end.

She sat as still as a carved figure, an elbow on the board and her chin in her cupped hand, contemplating something in her mind that made her eyes sombre.

She was not alone. Dame Bevinda, her mother, sat near her at the table-head, a tambour-frame* before her on the board below the light, and she was engaged in making careful stitches on some white circle of embroidery. So she had some of the arts of woman as well as of captain. Every now and then she glanced aside at her daughter, but her daughter never looked at her. Both were silent.

I could not stand watching there for ever. The man in the armoury, recovering wind, would be urgent to discover the hog that rid him of it ; the alarm might be expected any moment now. My only road led through this upper hall and through the bolted door behind the ladies' backs. Take it while there is time, David Gordon, and risk the Dame's alarm. So I drew in a deep breath, drew the curtain aside, and stepped softly within.

I was half-way down and within the circle of light when Eithne saw me. She did not start, but her eyes widened and narrowed and again widened, and she rose from her chair as if lifted by a force outside herself.

" David ! " she whispered, and her lips remained apart.

Dame Bevinda hid her surprise. She did not even rise from her chair, but leaned her hands on her tambour-frame and waited till I had halted before them. " And why the long blade, Master David ? " she inquired calmly.

I glanced down at my naked sword, and for the first time it looked a silly long weapon. I smiled at it and sheathed it quickly, and shook cloak loose on my arm.

* A small drum-like frame on which material was stretched for embroidering.

" That is more seemly, surely. Did you break through
your locked door ? How many dead men are behind you,
Blackcock's Feather ? "

" None yet, Dame."

" And now ? "

" I will take that door behind you, with your favour."

" And without it ? "

" Then I must take it without, Dame."

She laughed, not unkindly. " You know," she said, " I
will be sorry to see the last of you."

" Your sorrow may be long in coming, Dame," I gave
her back.

Eithne had been watching me with all her eyes, and
now she did a thing that surprised me. She jerked back
her chair and ran light-footed up the long room to the head
of the stairs leading down to the main hall. She leaned
there listening, her dark head turned aside, and the mother
and I watched her.

" You grow in daring, Master David," the Dame mused,
her eyes not turning to me. " Shall I look for you before
Saturday ? "

" Or after it, Dame."

" Then you will be late."

" No, by my word ! " I was driven to say—" as long as
a sword can cut a knot."

" A threat ? "

" Take it so."

" I take your dare, Blackcock's Feather."

Suddenly Eithne started, looked towards us, hesitated,
leaned again to listen, and then came flying to us, an arm
extended to me. " Fly, David ! " Urgent the whisper.
" They come."

And in turn her mother surprised me. She started up
from the chair. " Silly girl ! " she cried. " Could you
not think ? " She threw a word to me over her shoulder :
" Quick ! " and, long-striding, went up the hall and stepped

within the stair door. We heard her voice : " Your pardon,
Sir Francis. I was seeking a flagon of your sweet muscadine."

We did not catch the reply. We did not wait for it. Eithne
had my arm and was dragging me towards the side door,
too fast for dignity. " Hurry, hurry, David ! " Her strong
young hands were quicker on the bolt than mine, and the
cold air beat in on us through the open door.

I caught her two hands in mine. " I will be back, queen.
Listen, now ! Trust Donn Maguire and his friend O'Dwyer
—to the death."

" I know—I know ! Go now." Then she pushed me
quickly out in the dark and shut the door softly in my face.

I leaned against the parapet wall by the side door and
now I was out in the cold and unfriendly night.

Unfriendly ? No. A fine night for a venture like mine,
dark, but not dead black, with faint stars in the rents of a
sky ragged before a nor'th wind ; a bleak windy October
night with, now and then, a cold spit of rain in the wind's
mouth. There below me was Athenry, dark and still ; before
me in the dimness stretched the parapeted head of the east
wall, and all I had to do was to bend head below parapet
and make for the corner bastion and the north wall.

There at last was the loom of the bastion close ahead,
and I paused to peer and listen for the sentinel before ventur-
ing round by the glacis platform. The only sound was the
sough of the wind in the teeth of the parapet, and I was about
to slip round the body of the tower when a yellow spark of
light appeared far down the north wall. It swung a little
from side to side and came nearer as it swung, and as it came
nearer the tramp of footsteps came with it. The night patrol
changing guard. Many a wakeful night I had lain in my
quarters and listened to it tramping by every couple of hours,
and watched the lanthorn gleam run along the ceiling. I
slipped in behind the tower and waited for the sentinel's
challenge, but his challenge, when it came, startled me.
For it came from less than a score of feet away round the

curve of the wall. Very like, the careless fellow had been sheltering from the wind in the angle of the bastion, and it was my luck—and his too—that the patrol had halted me.

I listened anxiously. If Ned Billing was on his nightly round, he might, as was not unusual, circle the tower and seek the castle for a last drink. And I would not care to set Ned's loyalty and his friendship over against each other. But when the patrol halted at the other side of the bastion it was the sergeant's voice that was lifted. After that followed a murmuring and a shuffling ; then a brisk order, the quick stamp of trained feet, and the patrol moved away towards the north gate.

No sound once more but the piping of the wind, yet still I waited and listened—and in the end jumped too quickly to an explanation. " The sentinel," I told myself, " is gone up the wall behind the patrol ; now for it ! " And forthwith I darted round the tower—straight into his arms.

" Luck, the trickster, once again ! "

" Who goes—— "

He got no further. My cloak smothered him, and his arquebus dropped between us. I had not time to be gentle and apologetic. He was a thick short fellow, but already I had his head down in a notch of the parapet, a hand on his throat, my weight on his chest, and a knee across his thighs. A little jerk of pressure to warn him how easily his neck would snap, and he went limp under me. I pulled up his head then and put my mouth to his ear. " Silence or I kill ! "

I threw the cloak off his face and he must have caught my feathered bonnet against the sky. " Blackcock's Feather ! " whispered his strangled voice.

I was thinking rapidly and closely. My plan to drop from the wall into my old quarters and have word with Donn and Cathal would be possible only if I killed this man. And, cold-blooded, I could not kill him. Donn would

have word soon enough and would understand. The only
thing that remained was to drop into the ditch—and a
sufficiency of the fear of death into the sentinel to give me
time to get out of reach.

" Attend ! " said I in a deep growl, and the slack tremor
of him under my hands showed that he would welcome
mercy but did not expect it. " You will march up the wall
to the second culverin and there count two hundred—
slowly. Come back then and your arquebus will be here.
One small outcry, and I will throw your weapon into the
ditch—and you can explain how you lost it before they hang
you. Suit yourself. March ! "

And he marched. He had not gone fifty paces before
I grasped the pointed edge of the parapet, vaulted over,
let myself drop to full length, thrust feet against the stones
and leaped blindly. I struck ground with a jar and went
hands and knees amongst the dying weeds in the bottom of
the ditch. There were nettles too, I knew by the sting. On
my feet again, I groped forward to the back of the ditch.
It was a slope of stiff clay and I kicked in a toe-hold, clambered
to the top and faced round to Athenry.

There it lay hid in the night, fateful place of kings, fatal
field of Connacht, blown over by the wind, showing neither
tower nor roof, deeming itself safe against surprise.

And here was its doom looking in over its toothed sunken
north wall.

CHAPTER XXIX

THE STORMING OF ATHENRY

THE wind blew steadily out of the north, and I could not go astray by holding in the teeth of it. Before me was the empty spread of pasture-land, and beyond that, beech woods to the marshes of Suck ; and beyond Suck I must be before morning.

So, grasping cloak and sword under an arm, I struck the long slipping hillman gait, the hunter's lope that eats the miles. The keen wind sharpened me, the thin rain freshened me, the dark was a friend of mine. A strange new gaiety came over me. It was splendid to be free again. But an hour ago had I stared into the weary horror of the dungeon, and only now did I know how abasing to the soul is even the easiest of captivity. Here now was freedom and a purpose with it. Some time to-morrow I might strike the outposts of O'Donnell, gone to earth somewhere south of Cong, and the words I had to say to him would surely bring the eagles of the north swooping on Athenry. And then— and then ?

The wall of the woods loomed before me. In there was safety. And then somehow, of no will of my own, my voice lifted in our cheer for freedom—the long howl of the wolf on the run, that high quivering hair-bristling call of the killing trail. The trees echoed back that howl.

Soon I was forcing through thickets of bramble and hazel that fringed the open beech glades. The branches brushed dankly against my hands up to guard my eyes, briar trailers caught at my knees, grass tussocks were treacherous under my feet, but I pressed steadily forward, and at last won through to the leaf-carpeted open.

And there something caught my feet that was no briar, and I fell full-length on my face. Sudden hands caught my shoulder, a heavy body threw itself across my legs, a bent knee was in my back.

" Gay lad, we will put a stop to your howling ! "

Caught ! A moment ago free, with knowledge of the splendour of freedom—and now flat as a toad and as helpless.

A toad ? No ! a tod !* A fox lying still but not cowed. For, surely, if freedom was such a splendid thing it was worth fighting for—and dying for. Now ! this minute. If I had any of the fury of the Gael in me——.

" Quiet as a rabbit he is," said a deep voice above me, and hands slackened for an instant.

At that I jerked my shoulders free, embraced a hairy limb, and sent a body toppling. The man on my back fell over and I elbowed him fiercely in the ribs. " Manus, you pig, where are you ? " he roared. But for the man on my legs I might have torn clear, but before I could kick him off the other two pounced back on me.

Hands clawed, feet twined, blows clouted ; and striking, kicking, twisting, I heaved myself up, tangled in my cloak, sword between my legs. Twice I reached my knees, once my feet, and my hand on my hilt, but my attackers were as dourly determined as I was and again swarmed me down. Before I fell that last time I somersaulted a man over my shoulder, fell on him, and held him under me to die.

" Chief," roared a straining voice. " Will I prick him —or Ferdoragh is a dead man ? By the throat he has him."

" Hands off *scian* ! " commanded a voice outside the vortex. " Would you spoil our night ? Three of you to one man ! You sons of boors ! Give me room."

At his first words I stopped struggling. My fingers loosed from the man's neck, and I allowed myself to be dragged clear of him.

" Grip him, Manus," panted the deep voice, " or he is on us again. The mad wolf ! Ferdoragh's windpipe is broken, anyway."

* A fox.

" And what were your big paws doing, Teig ? " up-braided the chief's voice. " Put him on his feet, babes, and let me rest hand on him."

One of the men holding me suddenly caught me round the body and swung me upright. " There he is, then, and the devil is in it if he breaks this hold."

But my stark fury was burned out. In the reaction and relief, laughter came up in my throat.

" Bless us all ! The tears are at him," said an amazed growl at my shoulder. And at that I broke into a bark of laughter.

A tall figure loomed before me and a firm hand caught my shoulder. " Who laughs at death, fine fellow ? " he questioned me sternly.

" Time you asked," I said calmly.

His face came close. " Who is it ? "

" A pleasant welcome, cousin Donal," said I.

" Davy ! Is it you, my darling ? " His hands fell about my shoulders and ran up to my hair. I could feel the caress in them ; I was amongst my own again. " It is yourself," he whispered. " God is good."

Teig Ironhand loosed his clutch, but before he did, I felt his great palm press over my heart. " The hurt of hell to us ! " he cried. " There are a couple of splinters out of me, any-way." And then came a note of satisfaction into his voice : "And Ferdoragh is choked dead, my fine man ! "

" He was near that same," said Ferdoragh from the ground. " *Mhuire*, but I saw the gates of death in front of me."

We all laughed, and the throat-filling tension eased.

Donal Ballagh's arm was round me now. "A miracle under the stars," he said. " Senan will say it was his prayers. He is behind in the woods half a mile."

" But how are you here ? " I began to wonder.

" Looking for you, my light ; what else ? We knew where you were held. Where is Doncadh Donn ? "

" Back there in Athenry—and playing his part. A long story, cousin."

" Let us to where it can be told, then—with the night before us."

And so we went back to Donal's camp amongst the beeches, and waked Father Senan from his nest at the foot of a tree. And frankly he went over me and could not speak for a long time.

" We came down to look over the walls of Athenry," said Donal at last, " and maybe look inside them too."

" With how many men ? " I asked. " Remember what fell in Sligo, when I lost my bonny troop."

" Five only—God rest them—and Teig here with a small limp."

" It was worth it," said Teig, lying on the ground before us.

" I have two hundred of our own lads in these woods," said Donal. " Enough ? "

" Two hundred !   A thousand—— "

He caught my arm. "Listen, my heart o' corn! We are the spearhead only. Hugh Roe has three times your thousand strung out and across behind us—all moving softly and all pointing this way—waiting for the home-thrust. Enough ? "

I felt an excitement surge in me. " Donal," I cried, " if O'Donnell is bold as they say, he could storm Athenry this night."

" Bold !   Athenry is ours. Hugh Roe is not a mile behind. Let us back and talk to him."

Everyone has heard of the great sack of Athenry and of the fight that lasted from dawn to high noon. Hugh Roe O'Donnell deservedly gets fame for the exploit, but Hugh Roe himself gave Donal and me our full meed.

We had drawn up to the sunken north wall in the dark hour before the dawn, a spearhead of fifty men ; and ten times that number lay strung out on the plain before the north gate. Our forlorn hope of fifty was to make a surprise sally on the wall and on the gate-tower, with the intent of lifting the portcullis and letting the five hundred in ; and the five hundred, once in, would secure a hold on Athenry that might not be broken before the heavy-armed gallow-glasses came up from the camp beyond the marshes. After th it nothing could save that stronghold to the English.

Behold me, then, in the dark hour creeping to the brink of the ditch and looking in over the sunken wall. At my shoulder, his hand in my belt, was Donal Ballagh, and stretched out and linked behind us was a chain of fifty men. Each man carried on his shoulders a great bundle of grass and faggots. I had led that burdened chain across the plain from the woods, and it had been a most nerve-tightening task. For I had nothing to guide me but the wind, and one small shift in that would throw me wide of Athenry. Somehow I felt the hardest of my task over when the gate-tower loomed out of the darkness.

Donal and I crouched on the brink of the ditch and listened. There were no sounds but our breaths, our heart-thuds, and the wind piping as it always piped, careless of man and his affairs.

" We will be quiet," whispered Donal, " as long as the watch lets us."

I slipped into the ditch and Donal followed after a word to the man behind. And then we built our bridge of faggots, each man passing his bundle up the line and Teig Ironhand throwing it down to us.

The sentinel gave no sign while the work proceeded. He gave no sign when at last Donal, Teig and I crouched within the parapet close to a mounted culverin.

" They use a shelter-spot in the corner of the bastion down there," I explained.

" Wait you here," whispered back Teig. " It would be the fine thing to keep him quiet," and he crept up the wall.

We waited. No sound came out of the dark, but in less than five minutes Teig himself came crouching.

" He was asleep for himself," Teig told us simply. " So I

gave him one small clout and tied his belt in his teeth. Let us to it."

Donal and Teig sat astride, each in a notch of the parapet, and one by one the even flow of men was helped over into my hands. Our bridge gradually sank, and the last few men had to be hauled up from their own height below the wall. My part was to array the men in a close line along the shelter-wall towards the gate. No word was spoken ; the men came silently into my hands ; silently I led them into place ; and silently patted each man on the shoulder for a comrade. They were my own men and ready for any game.

The north wall was ours. And Athenry, confident of its strength, was in its last dawn sleep. Not yet was there the clang of steel, the yell of slogan, anything at all to warn it of its doom. The wind only, weary and never weary, cried with a mournful sameness.

Now I was moving forward, drawn sword in my left hand, my right touching now the parapet, now the chill flank of a culverin. Donal came close behind, his hand again in my belt, and behind him the linked line followed. The big mass of the gate-tower loomed above. My hand touched cold stone in front, and then the cut lintel of the guardroom door and, groping softly over wood, found the iron latch-guard. " Ready ! " I whispered and that small whisper sighed down the line.

The latch clicked, the door swung in, and quietly as a friendly visitor I stepped out of the dark into the murky light of the guardroom of the north gate.

I changed hilt to right hand.

The north gate of Athenry was defended by keep, draw-bridge, and portcullis ; and portcullis and draw-bridge were controlled from the guard-room wherein I now stood. This was a great chamber covering the whole floor of the keep ; east and west were doors giving on the wall head ; a row of window-slits looked in on Athenry ; and opposite these was the windlass with chains running through loop-holes in the wall. In a far corner was the door of the turret stairs leading to Ned Billing's quarters.

I strode in at the east door and got the whole scene at a glance : the red smoulder of the peats in the big fireplace, the smoky glow of the lanthorns on the wall, the grotesque shadows leaping into the darkness of the arched roof, the guard scattered at ease. The men—twenty or so—were at the hearth end and many of them asleep or dozing, sprawling on the wooden settles, leaning forward on the trestle-tables, lolling in the inglenook, unhelmeted, careless, dreaming no danger. And pouring in on them out of the dark a stream of fierce northern men, a gleam in their eyes and no worse gleam on the wicked blades of the axes.

One moment quietness and then—then we were amongst them. Someone lifted a head and cried shrilly—a bench fell crashing—a clamour lifted and was closed with the bellow of an arquebus—and steel rang on steel. Quick and short that fight ! The guard was surprised, and our men were built body and mind for hand-to-hand work. The press closed in, clanged, circled, broke asunder, scattered, and there was no more resistance.

Donal and I did not need to strike a single blow. The moment the fight broke, Donal and half a dozen picked men flung themselves on the windlasses, and the blows were still sounding when the chains of drawbridge and portcullis began to creak. For my own part, I was busy looking for Ned Billing, and swinging clear of the heart of the fight I made for the turret door. And I had almost reached it when it was jerked open and Ned burst through. He was mazed and barely awake, and his head without casque was round and nearly bald ; his tunic was unlaced and his broad chest showed through his linen ; and he carried his drawn sword in his right hand.

Just as he appeared, lean Ferdoragh, handy as a terrier, back-heeled a tall soldier before the turret door and had *scian* drawn back and down for the stroke. Billing with a

roar swung up his blade and slashed furiously downwards
at the clansman's head, but I took the blow close to the hilt
and jarred the sword out of his hand. Forthwith I strode
over Ferdoragh, got my forearm across Ned's throat and forced
him back into the doorway. Ferdoragh was behind me
yelling, " The *scian*, hero ! Give him the *scian* "—his short
red blade dancing and darting.

I looked at him over my shoulder. " Follow me," I shouted.

I had little time to spare, but that time could not be
better spent than in saving this veteran's life. I made full
use of my strength. I caught Billing round the small of the
back, and with one furious burst of energy bore him up the
stair and into his own sleeping-room. There I thrust him
backwards and brought blade to the point. Ferdoragh,
bundling in behind me, I collared left-handed.

Ned was still dazed. " David ! " he cried. " What is
it ? "

" The sack of Athenry," I told him. " You are my
prisoner."

He struck his breast with clenched fist. " Ah ! why did
you not let me die ? "

" Die ! " I bellowed. " Enough will die this day. Gather
your wits, man." I glanced down at Ferdoragh, now quiet
under my hand. " Ferdoragh, this man has befriended me
greatly," I said quietly.

" And me too, then," cried Ferdoragh, and grinned
happily after the manner of his breed. " And he after trying
to knock a hole in the poll of me."

" You will guard him here—with your life."

" With my life surely," said Ferdoragh soberly.

I turned and leaped for the door. " Do not be an old
fool, Ned ! " I threw over my shoulder. I heard the echoing
slogan of the clans in the arch.

High noon in Athenry and the fight in a dead-lock.

A long and swaying fight since the dawn, and at high
noon that dawn seemed far away. It had been a dawn that

came slowly. Slowly the wan day had lifted and broadened, showing pointed gables in one flat perspective with the great keep of the castle towering above, the grey of the stone walls, the black squares of windows, men lurking, soldiers running, smoke curling—and the fight worrying and thudding through it all.

Fearfeasa O'Clery the Bard made a song of the Sack of Athenry, and I have heard Turlough Mac an Teaclan sing it to the *clairseach* to bring the whole red fight back to one. He put into it the whirlwind onslaught of the clans, the high-breasted stand of the Sassenach, the stamp and sway and tongueless yelling of men, the shiver and gleam of steel, the first bright lift of the blade and the second dulled with killing, and behind all the great surging note of triumph. It is a grand song, and women hate it.

Let it be said here that the English and loyalist Irish met our onslaught with a fierce starkness worthy of all great fights. Hurriedly mustered out of barrack and bothy, they uprose behind walls, leaped down on us from embrasures, leaned to fire from window and roof, manned here and there a hurried barricade, and in the end held us in lock before half the town was won.

My part in that fight was that of all the others of my breed ; breast to breast, driving inwards shoulder to shoulder, desperately eager and determined unto death to secure a hold on Athenry that could not be shaken till the gallowglasses came. We had won East Lane and the whole length of the north wall, and had come up starkly against an iron resistance along the square at the heart of the town. A score of us had won across a lane making two triangles of Athenry and were attacking a stone house strongly held. We flanked it down a narrow alley between head-high walls, and Teig Ironhand, who had fought shoulder to shoulder with me all that morning, gave me a heel lift to the crown of the wall on the right. As I bent to tug him up, the whole world crashed to blankness before my eyes ; a clang, a flash, and I fell and fell into utter darkness. It was that sudden bending sideways that had saved my life ; for as I bent, an arquebus ball grazed above my ear and laid me senseless outside the wall.

CHAPTER XXX

THE IRISH CHIEF AND THE WOUNDED CHAMPION

IT had been a sore clout on a hard Scots head, and it was long and long before my senses returned to their citadel. Consciousness came out of the well of blackness, trembled on the edge, dipped back and came again. I looked up and men who were strange bent over me, and I wondered where and who I was. It was night-time, I knew, for candles burned on the wall where the arras was torn and branches of laurel and holly glistened here and there. It was the branches of ever-green that, queerly enough, brought memory back. This was the upper hall of Athenry castle decked for the feast—but why were the green leaves draggled and the arras torn ? And a smell of smoke and burning was in my nostrils.

" Eithne ! " said I aloud, and my voice was heavy and tired.

" Give him a drink," said a voice I knew, and I looked at the men around me. They were strangers no longer. Father Senan sat on the edge of the stretcher-couch whereon I lay on my back ; Donal Ballagh and Teig bent over his shoulder, and Ned Billing stood at the other side, a flagon cupped in his hand.

" Father ! " said I.

" Son ! " said the priest, and his hand was cool on mine.

Teig's bearded face crinkled up as if tears would flow, but, instead, he laughed. " Man alive ! " said he warmly. " You could not kill him ! "

" Not with a stone head," said Ned Billing.

Donal Ballagh drew his hand downwards from brow to chin, and his face that had been white and strained was now smiling. He could not say a word, but his eyes told me his liking.

And then I knew the dull throb of an ache above my right ear and felt the tightness of a bandage across my brow. I brought a hand up to feel and winced at the twinge.

" Fine ! " said Donal with satisfaction. " Good and fine ! Now we know that you are back to us."

They gave me the drink that I needed. Teig wanted to give me ale as the only safe drink to quench a grown man's thirst, but the old friar knew enough of wounds and medicines to insist on cool water. After that I was able to turn on my side and get an elbow under me, though the room rocked. " Did anyone see my good bonnet ? " I asked.

" Here it is," said Donal, " with the devil's horns still on it—and the dint in the steel mesh that saved you."

I looked around the hall. There was no one in it but ourselves. " Athenry—— "

" Is ours. It is so ! When the gallowglasses came we burned down the wooden doors and in on them."

" Prisoners ? "

" A few. Your Sir Francis Vaughan with a broken thigh-bone—and this officer you left with Ferdoragh."

I looked at Ned Billing and reached him my hand. " Donal," said I, " this is Captain Ned Billing and my friend."

" We knew that. We hope he will like a winter at Dungiven ! "

I looked up at Donal, but Donal would not look at me. It was Senan that told me, still holding my hand. " The Governor sent the women out to safety before the gallow-glasses came—to Athlone, we think. She is not in town, David—nor is Donn Maguire, dead or alive."

I lay back on the stretcher. There was no more I wanted to know. My bright bird, so near my hand, had flown away or been caged away and the winning of Athenry was only an empty boast. I was weak and weary and aching. Life was too

low in me to feel the stab. I shut my eyes and was dumb—
dumb as a fish and as cold.

That night in the upper hall of Athenry was a thousand
years long. And in time I was no longer cold. My head
grew hot and throbbing, and disjointed fragments of dreams
came and went tormentingly. Then the darkness began to
tremor all round me, and a strange sensation of size, yet
lightness, came over me, my head seemed to grow and grow
and be too immense for any neck to bear ; some mystic inward vision had an illusion of looking on a smooth snow-white
ocean, that moved evenly at first, then broke into chaos across
the width of the world ; every least sound was magnified and
full of horror ; my breathing filled the bowl of the sky ; the
rustle of the torn arras was more terrible than thunder·;
great weights fell and rolled, great seas swept and broke,
and made no sound ; a weird radiance that came from
neither sun nor moon threw no shadow ; and I was alone
in that chaos where some unnamable disaster had overcome
earth and sky and the kingdom of God. There was no time
any more, and I was so lost in my doom of nothingness that I
had forgotten the memory of men. And yet, through it all, I
knew that I lay in the upper hall of Athenry suffering only
from a child's nightmare of eternity.

And then suddenly came quietness, and someone was
speaking close to me—a hoarse voice gabbling words I could
not catch. I listened intently and the voice stopped, and with
a shock I realised that myself was the speaker. Father Senan's
arm was under my shoulder and his flagon of cool water at
my lips.

" Fine you will be the morn, small son," murmured the
gentle rumble of his voice.

" The grey morn," wondered I—" must it always come ? "

" And the sun with it—God bless us all. Lie quiet now,
Davy."

Donal and Teig, great strong men weary after the long
fight, slept leagues deep on the floor near me ; but the old

friar who, not fighting, had been busy all day at his own high work among the dying, did not sleep at all. If I groaned, if I dreamed aloud, if I flung restlessly, he was at my side, wetting my dry lips, moistening the bandages on my brow, crooning over me the words that a mother croons to her sick child.

In the grey dawn he washed out the gash above my ear with sour wine and put on a fresh bandage, and then gave me a long drink that had in it a thin lacing of Bordeaux wine. And after that peace came and I drifted into sleep, drifted deep and deep and had no dreams.

It was high day when I waked, and a bar of sunlight lay across the cloak that covered me. The heat and ache were out of my bones, and only a small dull ache in my head— and I was hungry. I turned over and lifted on my elbow. " Will anyone give me my yesterday's breakfast ? " I wanted to know sourly. And a fine peal of laughter went up to the arches.

Hugh Roe O'Donnell our great leader stood at my side with Donal and the priest. Slim and fine he was, a clean silken tunic on his supple shoulders and his red hair smooth above the clean pallor of his face. And a smile hid the dream-gloom in his grey eyes. " Breakfast it is," he cried, " or I go without."

I felt embarrassed and had no word to say.

" He will take what he gets," said Senan, " and it will be fat enough for him."

The prince put his hand on my shoulder and I felt the warmth of his fingers. " David Gordon," said he, " the North owes you a great victory." I moved my heavy head slowly, and he bent and looking into my eyes smiled wistfully. " I know—I know, friend of my heart ! " he said slowly. " I cannot help you. What you want you must take with your own hands. My fine lad ! my poor lad ! But what is O'Donnell's is yours always." He touched me softly on the shoulder, turned and walked away slowly, his hands behind him and his head forward—a young but very lonely man. And we all were silent till he passed through the door.

I put a long leg out of the bed. " If you think—— "

Donal put me back with one hand. " Here comes your breakfast, red fellow."

Teig came with a bowl of porridge—gruel it was and steaming, with a horn spoon in it and a bare lick of honey on it.

" No ! " I roared, and looked at Senan. " Is this all I am getting, bald pate ? "

"Just that." His eye was obdurate, and I looked at Donal who kept a serious face.

I took the bowl roughly from Teig's great hands, looked at it with disgust, and : " Very well so," I growled. " I may as well try it." And they laughed at me.

The spoon was angry against the bottom of the bowl. " Give me a drink," I commanded and they hurried me a full flagon of milk.

" There is water in this," I complained in the middle.

" No, child ! " protested the priest. " Only the poor Connacht cows."

Again I put a leg over the side and this time the priest stopped me : " Let me see that cut, son."

He was pleased with it ; there was little poison there, he said, and he bandaged it afresh. Teig shaved off my red stubble, and I grumbled when he rasped me. Donal sat silently at the end of the stretcher and waited till my face was dry, and then he looked into my eyes, felt my hand, and nodded. " David," said he then, " there is a dying man wants word with you."

" Not Donn—— "

" No—no ! Donn is whipped off to Athlone, I doubt. A man in your lodging—— "

" Cathal O'Dwyer ? "

" It could be. He has the Leinster tongue. He is dying, I fear."

" Dying ? "

" Shot through the body."

" Who did it ? "

" He will not say. All he will say is : ' Bring me David Gordon—I will see David Gordon '—and he is holding his life with his two hands."

" Is Cosby of Cong here ? "

" No—not in Athenry, dead or alive."

My poor Cathal ! He had failed in his vengeance and now, dying, it still possessed him and he would bequeath it to me. Cosby, no doubt, had guarded the women to Athlone. I was tired of Cosby. I had no desire any more to hold him at sword-point. But O'Dwyer was my true friend and must be seen. And whatever task he might put on me, that would I do—or die.

I was staggering on long unstable legs and Donal had an arm round me. " I will see him," I insisted.

They helped me on with my clothes, and we went out on the east wall, Donal on the glacis-side and holding my arm, Teig and the priest behind. It was again a fine brisk October morning, with the sun in a high frail sky and an east wind blowing the smoke away from us. Athenry was still smouldering. Here and there a stone house stood, but all the clay and wooden bothies were burned down to fragments of walls and smoking litter. The kerns were busy searching out spoil, but the main force of gallowglasses were camped in the plain outside the castle, and a great drove of cattle was being already herded northwards towards the woods. The houses below the north wall where the culverin had been heaved into the ditch were still whole, this part of the place having been taken in the first onfall, and the house of the Welshwoman our landlady had not even been looted.

She came hurrying down from the attic and was glad to see me. She too, had grown fond of Cathal O'Dwyer— he was so quiet and gentle, she said, and gave no trouble. " He is dying, Master Gordon," she told me. " There is no more blood in him."

Donal helped me to his door and left me, and, as one should do in a chamber of death, I took off my bonnet as I entered.

CHAPTER XXXI

A MESSAGE FROM EITHNE

CATHAL was lying under his cloak on the trestle-bed and I thought he was already dead. There was no colour in him, not even on his lips, and the bones of his face stood out against the drawn skin. But that face was set austerely, invincibly, in some proud calm of its own, stronger than death's calm ; and those steadfast eyes could not be blinded by the blank stare of death. Whatever was behind that unhuman calm was secure beyond all doubt, held more firmly than by stone walls. His hands clasped each other across his breast, and the knuckle-bones stood out like strong bosses.

I tiptoed to the bedside and then his eyes moved and turned on me, and though his face never changed, his eyes smiled. I sank down beside him on my knees. " Cathal, Cathal, my brother," I whispered. " Who hurt you ? "

" Brother too." His lips formed the words, and I held my ears close. " Be not minding that now." Every word was quietly slow and drawn carefully. " All is well with me at last. My heart broke in me that day in Dublin—and Cathal O'Dwyer was only a dead man, not resting. I want you to listen to me now, for there is not much time, and I am keeping Colum waiting for me over there." His eyes sought the foot of the bed, and my hair lifted.

" Listen, David. Donn Maguire was taken to the castle last night, and this is the message that he sent to me for you by a woman Breadh : ' The one you know will be waiting for you in the Glen of the Echo, and a message will be waiting for you in the township of Bellaghy.' Say that after me. ' The one you know—— ''

I said it word for word, and content warmed his cold eyes.

" My work is done at last," he whispered.

" No, Cathal, no ! Who did this to you ? "

" Searching for you, he found me here——' "

" Cosby ? "

" But it was the good turn he did me—me, a dead man walking. Listen now again, brother. All that seeking of mine was folly. Let it stop with me. I take back your word. Do not you be minding Cosby. He and you and I are in the hands of God, and let us not be struggling in that nest. Are you heeding me ? "

" I am." But, indeed, I was not.

He looked at me long. "Ah, well ! I can do no more." His voice came strong. " I will come now, O'More."

His hands loosed and one of them sought mine. It was colder than clay but the fingers pressed mine firmly. And then he died. The life he had held so calmly strong went out of him, quieter than a breath. I did not know that he was dead yet awhile. His face did not change, his breath made no sound, his eyes were as calm as the sky. Then his lips parted and his fingers loosed, and I knew that he was gone.

I stood looking down at him, and his death possessed me. For all the advice that he had given me my mind was set on him, on the bitterness of his days and the pity of his death. He was better at rest. Surely his heart was broken that day in Dublin, and he had been no more than a ghost driven by an urge that in the end failed. I felt extraordinarily bitter. This man had been treated unfairly—by fate and by man. By man ! by one man. In my mind's eye I saw the tossed flaxen hair of Cosby and his pale eyes and his mouth laughing without humour. And with that face in mind my teeth grated and I had no prayer to say.

I walked out of the room and found my three friends at the head of the stairs, and the Welshwoman on the steps below them.

" He is dead," I told them through shut teeth.

The woman threw her hands wide and opened her mouth to keen.

" Be quiet, woman ! " I stopped her savagely. " He is happier than you are who will have no house over your head the morn."

That stopped her. Her mouth remained open and it was no wider than her eyes.

" Be not worrying, woman-of-the-house," Donal comforted her. " This house and all in it will be safe."

The old priest was watching me with anxious looks. " I am sorry, Senan," I said to him, " there was not time."

" I saw him this morning early," said he. " Did you get his word ? "

" It can wait," said I shortly, and went down the stairs.

But on the crown of the wall the three of them came round me so that I could not move. They were very gentle and firm as good men are with a sick child. Fine they knew that the dead man's word concerned me closely, and they knew that in my then state I was not fit to handle it.

" What is it, cousin ? " Donal asked, his hand on me.

" Will any of you tell me where I can find Cosby ? " I asked back. I am not an obstinate man nor am I a vindictive one, but the clout on the head must have been working on me. It set all my humour on one road and closed down on that.

" Did the message concern Cosby ? " the priest queried quickly.

" He is my concern now. I will find him under the mountains at the World's End."

" Then what was the word you had, my light ? "

And strangely enough, I found it difficult to recall to mind the message that should have stirred me like a trumpet. I ran my hand over my bandaged brow and a change of mood came over me. " I am sorry, friends of my heart. You should not be troubling about me. Why are you so patient ?— but—but I will be better to-morrow."

" What did the dead man say to you, jewel of my heart ? "

I looked at the old man and said my piece carefully as I remembered it : " The word was from Donn Maguire, and it was that a message would be waiting for me in the township of Bellaghy, and that one I know would be waiting for me in the Glen of the Echo."

" Christ and Him risen ! " prayed the priest. " I knew it."

After that the three of them took no notice of me for a while. I might not have been there. They closed in and talked and I stood leaning against the shelter-wall, my eyes on the ground, and little fumes of hot mist curling across my sight. And I paid but little heed to what they said about a man that, somehow, was a stranger to me.

The thing that had to be done had to be done at once— Donal was certain of that. If Ormonde in Dublin had sent an army to Clifford or a fleet came round to Galway, Hugh Roe would avoid that scissors-hold and fall back on the north. There was no time to lose and to-day there was an open road. Then take your two hundred—this was Teig—and the O'Flaherty will not be ferocious. Father Senan was wiser. That would be a waste of time. A big force must go round head of Corrib, and there was no need for fighting. The way was open across the loch, and a few men moving boldly would be credited with strength behind them. A few men ! The fewer the better, said Donal, and that few here—but would the man be fit to ride ? Fit as he would be for a week—and a week was a year—and a man with a head like that was not a child to be killed——

But I was thinking thoughts of my own and suddenly cried out. " If you will not tell me, Vaughan will. I will go to Vaughan."

They had to give me my way that far.

We found Vaughan in his own quarters above the arch, lying comfortably enough on his own bed. Ned Billing opened the door to us. A skilled bone-setter of O'Donnell's had joined the broken bones, and one leg was a thick packet of splints and linen strips. Vaughan's face was pale and weary, but the sound strong bones of cheek and jaw had not weakened. He greeted me with a smile as I bent close and looked into his eyes. " Out of the wilderness ye again smote us ! " he murmured.

" Tell me, fine man of the English," I put to him, " why would you and I be always hurting each other ? "

" Because one of us was on the wrong side, my friend. It is our luck." He caught my sleeve and drew me nearer. " I missed your Ferrara early in the evening. Tom Pybus was killed in the fight."

" Ah—ah ! I was the death of him the fourth time. Will God judge him kindly ? "

" His meed." He drew me still closer. " There is something I should like you to know. Dame Bevinda is not gone to Athlone. She has taken herself and her retinue back to Corrib. You will know—— "

" I know nothing now till I find the man Cosby. Where is he ? "

He did not answer me for a long time.

" Friend," said I, " if you know, you will not hide it from me this hour."

" Where your lady is he will not be far away."

" It is so then ? " I turned to Donal behind me. " I will come with you now, cousin. Where is my sword ? "

CHAPTER XXXII

AT LAST !

I HAVE no clear memory of that second ride to Corrib, for I was out of my head all that day and some of the next. First I made a pother because they mounted me on a strange horse instead of on my own mare Benmee, and they had to be very patient in persuading me that she had been killed before Sligo.

" Sligo ! but that was a long time ago," I wondered. " I was there, and Teig here was singing a fine song."

" I was so," agreed Teig, " and I wearing a blackcock's feather."

" Were you now ? " I felt my own. " Am I Teig, or are you ? "

" Brothers, surely."

" Let that stand."

So I mounted the strange horse and off we set, the four of us, Father Senan leading, and Donal and Teig at either side of my crupper.

They tell me that I said no word all that ride till we came to the township of Bellaghy ; that I let my reins hang loose so that Donal had to touch my horse occasionally to keep it on the road, and that over and over, endlessly, I kept whistling a small piece of a gay tune that they had never heard before, but that I could never get the turn of it right—until at last Donal found himself whistling with me and lifting to the turn, and going off the tune in the same way.

It was near dark when we came to Bellaghy hamlet, but no man waited there for us with a message. They decided to stay there that night and Murrigan O'Flaherty Dhu gave us a kindly welcome. He knew who we were by now and his hospitality was no less because of that.

All I remember clearly of Bellaghy is that I did not sleep in it that night. Still I had sense enough to lie quiet in the dark and not trouble the old friar, who lay near me. Twice in the night I felt his hand on me, and once he put on a cool fresh bandage. In the dawn, when he was sleeping, I went out into the morning, but my head was too heavy and dazed to be cleared, even by the fresh dawn wind.

As I stood barelegged out in the open a dog barked and a man in a hurry came in at the other end of the village, a mountain man without cloak or head-covering. I waited for him, but he stopped a good ten paces away, as was only natural considering my appearance. " Is one David Gordon in this place ? " he called.

" David Gordon ! I do think that the ugly man is here somewhere—there was a message for him."

" It is with me."

" Wait now and I will see."

I turned, and there was Father Senan in the door. " There is a message for David Gordon," I explained. " Where—— ? Oh ! But am I not that fellow ? "

The mountain man was frightened and doubtful. " God be good to us all ! " he prayed.

" All is well, my son," the priest encouraged him. " What is your message."

" There is a boat waiting, and I am to take you to the mouth of the Glosha—and after that you will go where you know. There is hurry."

" We will go, then," said the priest.

So we crossed the loch, a sheen of silver in that still fall day, but I had no eyes for the lovely islanded wide reaches of the bay of Cong. They were fixed downwards on the hide bottom of the coracle, and I kept dully wondering if this stream of Glosha we were seeking flowed down out of Glen Rinnes—no ! Glounamaol—but where then was the Glen of the Echo that I had in my dreams ?

Going up the burn-side I was sore puzzled. " Why am I

here ? " I wondered aloud. " This way leads to a land of youth hid in the wilderness—and that is no place for a man in torment—nor for a cheerless laughter. Cosby is never in this place. This place is for quiet, not for drawn swords and the chill song of them. I was here aforetime with one I know— and there was a man fine-hearted who thought he could fish—— "

" True for you, son," murmured the priest. " He only thought it."

" That is he speaking, Senan, fisher of men."

" God bring us luck at the end of this road," prayed he troubledly, " or someone will be in the dark valley."

In time we came up over the tilt of Glounamaol into the mouth of the Glen of the Echo, and there the priest put his shoulder back against my breast, halting me, and Donal and Teig bunched close to us. " A wasps' nest we are landed in," cried Donal. " See the crowd at the bothy ? "

" Not more than half a score," said Teig of the long sight.

But I could not see all that distance. The great slopes of hill shimmered and danced before my eyes ; above the purple hump of Maam the loop of a rainbow twisted and twined tormentingly across the sky, and ribbons of hot vapour curled up out of the valley where the singing of the water was sadder than dreams.

" We should not be here," I whispered, " but let us on. There is a valley of stones beyond that will suit us better— where we can hide till brain burns cold. Hush ! here is the Echo-point, and the happy people might hear us."

" Up with us ! " cried Donal in his indomitable clarion voice. " Let us remember our clan and our name. We carry this thing through—or die. March on ! "

We marched on and made no pause till we came up on the green level before the bothy. There we halted.

Dame Bevinda was there and with her Duvesa Mac-Theobald of the dove hair and ten men of the O'Flaherty clan. The deer-flaying gallows had been knocked over and riven apart, and the men were gathered round one of its limbs; they were about to use it as a ram to batter down the bothy door. The old warden Garrodh had apparently locked it and gone away.

But at that time I did not see the Dame or Duvesa or the men about their ram. All I saw was Cosby. He was there !

I turned to Donal and placed a hand against his breast. " Donal," said I, " do not let anybody stop me."

He says my eyes that used be brown had turned yellow deep under brow and that the bosses of my cheeks had become hard marble.

" Cousin, dear," I said again, " do not let anybody stop me."

" No one under the sky," he said, iron in his voice.

" You were my own always," I said in my throat.

I swung away from him, and Andrea Ferrara came out in the light of the sun. Someone had cleaned it after the sack of Athenry and now it shone with a blue happy wickedness, and it whimpered shrill as it came from scabbard. Oh ! but the cold song of it made me strong and light as a leopard. I spurned the ground; when my feet lifted they did not want to come to earth again. Donal tells me that, in truth, I swayed from knee to shoulder and moved forward like a man weary and in no hurry, but that my face and the look in my eyes would frighten the Fianna ; that men shrank aside from me and no hand went to blade. And there was Dame Bevinda O'Flaherty before me.

" Would you dare to the end, Gordon ? " said she.

" Woman of the great heart," said I, " this thing had to be. Forgive me now."

Gently I put her aside with one hand, and there was Cosby facing me and his sword still in sheath.

" We meet for the last time, Captain Sir William Cosby," I said, giving him his full title. " It was meant from the day you slew my friend. Draw your sword."

He stood looking at me out of his light eyes, his teeth showing mirthlessly.

" Oh, cheerless laughter ! " I cried. " Laugh now. This is the end of all roads. Make your peace with Colum O'More and Cathal O'Dwyer. With me you make no peace on top of earth. Draw ! "

It happened very quickly. He saw me there swaying on my feet, head bandaged, face dead white, sword lax in my hand. Now was his time to kill. They say his blade came out in one mighty sweep and in the same motion slashed like a streak at my neck. But to me that blade was slow as sway of a branch in the wind and as soft as the stroke of a reed. I had to wait for it until it came from behind his shoulder. And there my blade locked on it like a curl of light, twisted over and under it, and leaped forward in one clean shoulder-driven lunge—through open mouth and through spine. The guard jarred against his teeth. He fell backwards. I recovered blade with a single wrench, and swung on the O'Flaherty men.

" Who dies now ? "

No one made the smallest move. It was all over.

I waited. A great weakness flowed over me ; the world rocked ; hilt slipped from loosed fingers ; I should have fallen. But it was as if a clean strong wind came about me to hold me up. A rustle of skirts, a cry, a pair of strong young arms, and there was my Eithne holding me.

" David—David ! "

I placed arm round her shoulder and leaned on her.

" Eithne," I cried, " I was needing you. It is you I am needing. Do not let them hurt me any more."

" No more, dear. No one—no one will hurt you any more."

Dame Bevinda had the last word.

" Sad day ! " she cried. " Sad day when the O'Flahertys are dared on their own ground. They need a man. Let it be."